Getting Lucky

Monstrous Rochester Book Two

Jessica Olin

For Jake B., my platonic life mate and heart sibling. If you read this book, don't tell me. There's a lot of sex in it.

Chapter One

I clicked the *Save* button and let out a long breath. That was it. My grades were submitted and my first year on the tenure track was officially over. It was anticlimactic, but it felt good.

I looked around my studio apartment and smiled at nobody in particular. As hard as I'd been working for this moment, having nothing to do next left me feeling at loose ends. Then I realized finishing this early in the evening meant I could meet my colleagues out for an end of year drink. My smile broadened. I had never felt comfortable going before, no matter how many times they'd tried to tell me that adjuncts were welcome. But I wasn't an adjunct. Not anymore.

Once my laptop was powered down and stored, I paused for a moment in the bathroom to take in my appearance. The woman in the mirror was looking a little too much like my mother for my comfort, so I took a moment to add some mascara and lip stain. Satisfied with my face, I fluffed up my curls with some product, then nodded. Not bad. I looked at my outfit, a printed but low-cut T-shirt and jeans that fit me flatteringly. Not the worst outfit for a casual drink out with friends, so I didn't change.

I grabbed my phone, my purse, and my keys, and was out the door.

> I can come after all. Where am I heading?

I sent to my friend Kim, one of the few other Jews besides me at the small Christian college where we both worked. I liked him, even if he was always trying to get me to attend singles night at his synagogue.

The answer came back before I had gotten all the way down to the parking lot.

> The Warren. I'll come get you out front if you text me when you arrive. Excited you're coming after all!

I smiled down at my phone and practically ran the rest of the way to my car.

Once I'd arrived and texted, I was greeted at the front door by Kim, his husband Dave, and another member of the English department faculty—Angela. They all had big grins on their faces as I walked up.

"So, your first year is over other than submitting grades. What do you have to say now, Niss?" Kim called out to me.

I opened my mouth to answer, but Angela cut in.

"It's not like it's really her first year. She adjuncted for Pittsford for, what, nine years prior to this?" She laughed.

I threw my shoulders back and affected a strut. "My grades are submitted."

"Kiss up." Kim laughed.

"Hey, you're the one who told me that getting my grades in right away would make me look good!" I grinned at them. "So, are we going to go in? I've been wanting to come here ever since Angela told me about it."

The Warren wasn't just one bar. It was four bars/restaurants, with the same menu but different settings, that were interconnected like a rabbit warren. They were supposed to have amazing hot wings. It had opened about nine months prior, and was doing well if the full parking lot was anything to judge by, but I hadn't come here yet. Until recently, I hadn't felt comfortable spending money on anything but the necessities. A little over a decade of barely scraping by ingrained habits in a person.

Angela hooked her arm through mine and pulled me towards the front door. Once we crossed the threshold, the group traced a weird and circuitous route through three different bar setups until we arrived at one that looked a lot like an Irish pub. It was busier than I would have expected for a Monday evening. I hoped that was a good sign.

Angela leaned in and whispered, "I'm sorry about this thing that's about to happen. I tried to talk him out of it."

I only half heard what Angela said. I was too busy looking at the bartender—a tall, strong woman with the sleeves of her button-down shirt rolled up to show one tattooed forearm and one freckled forearm. The bartender had red hair in a pushed back undercut, with a strip of white going up from her widow's peak. She winked at me when she noticed me watching. Drooling might be a more accurate description. I blushed and winked back at her.

I replayed what Angela had just said in my mind.

"Wait, what?"

As I watched, Kim dragged a tall, bespectacled man over to where Angela and I were standing. The grin on Kim's face was a little unnatural, forced. "Janice Rose, this is my friend, Samuel Epstein. Sam, this is Niss."

Sam reached out a hand for me to shake. He looked as confused as I felt.

"Sam is the new head of education at our synagogue and has only lived in the Rochester area for about six months. Niss works with me and Angela, who you already met, at Pittsford College in the English department." Kim's grin got so big it almost looked like it was going to swallow the rest of his face, Cheshire Cat style. "And you're both single."

Having made that pronouncement, Kim pulled Angela and Dave away, leaving me still awkwardly holding hands with Sam.

I let go and had to force myself not to wipe my hand against my jeans. Much as I was disconcerted by the situation, there was nothing wrong with Sam.

"I swear I had no idea he was going to do that. I wasn't even sure why Kim invited me to this bar tonight, but he's a decent guy who was on the committee that hired me, so I came anyway," Sam said. The man looked desperately uncomfortable, so I was inclined to believe him. "I attended one singles event at the synagogue a few months ago, which was a mistake because now everyone is trying to set me up with any single Jewish woman between the ages of twenty-five and sixty-five."

I shrugged. "I split the difference at forty-five."

"Me, too." Sam gave me a crooked smile that made him more appealing. "Then I made an announcement that I wasn't willing to date anyone who went to Temple B'nai B'rith or was related to anyone who attended. I thought they'd given up." He looked over his shoulder at Kim, who'd been joined by a couple other members of the faculty. I recognized one as a history professor who'd started on the tenure track this year as well, and the other was someone I'd only seen at faculty meetings. "I should have known better."

"I'm one of those agnostic verging on atheistic Jewish types. Though I did pick up a book about Jewish folklore and another about the Mussar movement at the bookstore the other day." I figured I *was* single and he wasn't bad looking. And it had been a long while since anyone but me had gotten me off. It wouldn't hurt to chat with the man.

"Mussar, huh? That's some deep stuff. Are you normally into philosophy or was this just a one off?" Sam grinned and I took a moment to look at him. I could do worse, so I threw myself into the conversation.

An hour later, I knew that Sam was five months older than me, divorced, and the father to two college-aged boys. I knew he'd been divorced for four years and had moved to the Rochester area to be closer to his aging parents. I also knew there wasn't a spark for me, but that wasn't the end of the world when dating in middle age. I was at a point in my life where I'd admitted to myself a good night's sleep and political compatibility were more important than a sexual spark. Besides, I had quality toys. What I didn't have was companionship outside of my work colleagues and my parents.

Then Sam had to go—he had work in the morning—so we exchanged phone numbers but made no firm plans to meet up again.

Once he was gone, Kim and Dave rushed over to my table. Angela trailed after them. "Well?" Kim asked. "He's a cutie, isn't he? I told Dave that if Sam weren't straight, he might be in trouble."

Angela rolled her eyes, which was exactly how I felt.

"I told him that he'd have competition," Dave responded, but he wasn't looking at me. He was staring, heart in his eyes, at his husband. Then he kissed Kim's temple. I liked not being the only Jew at work, but I liked not being the only queer even better. This was a bit much, though.

But people who are in love want everyone to be in love, so I decided to be generous. "He was nice enough, and yeah, he is good-looking." I swallowed the last of my wine. "Not sure if anything will come of it, but it was fun to chat with him."

"Well, you'll have time. You do have all your grades in, after all." Angela bumped my shoulder and grinned.

"Not that much time. I'm teaching all three summer sessions. But I am going to enjoy the couple of weeks between here and the start of the first one. Going to try to sleep in, and I might even read a book for pleasure in between prepping my classes."

Dave's phone rang, and he stepped away from the group.

Angela picked the conversation back up. "I'm not teaching until the second session, and only under protest. I shouldn't complain since the money will be nice, but I need some time off."

"Yeah, I need time off, too, but I need the money more." I shrugged, then laughed. "Oof, I think that last glass of wine might not have been a great idea. I'm definitely tipsy now." I laughed again.

"Hon, we need to get going." Dave put his phone away as he returned. "Babysitter called to say she's not feeling well and needs to go home. Rotten luck."

"Crap," Kim said.

"Crap," Angela echoed. "They're my ride." She looked around. "I think most everyone else came in for one drink and left before you even got here. Means we're leaving you on your own. You going to be okay? I can call you a ride share if you want."

I shook my head. "I'll have some water and read one of the many books I have on my phone. Maybe I'll even get some of those hot wings. Give myself some time to sober up. If that doesn't work, I'll call myself a taxi. But thanks."

There were hugs all around, and when I had seen them off I made my way to the bar. The stools there looked comfortable. Besides, this way I could stare at the sexy bartender. No sooner had I sat than she was putting a coaster in front of me. I looked up and was once again dazzled by the gorgeous woman. Even in the dimness of the bar, her hair caught the light and looked like fire. The way her eyes crinkled when she smiled made me want to smile back. I'd always had a thing for butch redheads, and she was ticking all my boxes.

"More Riesling?" the woman asked, her voice deep and rich. I felt her gaze like a caress. This, I thought, was what a spark felt like.

I leaned forward. "I'm going to need to drive, so no thanks. I'll take a seltzer with a lime. Anyway, how do you know what I was drinking? A waitress delivered all my wine tonight. Do you always pay such close attention to what everyone drinks?"

"Only when the person drinking is really pretty." The grin the bartender gave me said the other woman knew she was being cheesy. Up close, I could see she had light freckles across her cheeks and nose and a few down her neck. God, I was a sucker for freckles. I wondered how far down they went. "How would you feel about a virgin mojito? Pretty much what you asked for, but with muddled mint and some sugar."

"That sounds amazing, actually. I'd love it."

The bar had emptied out somewhat. I felt a little awkward watching the bartender so closely, but then again, how often did I get to watch a master at work?

"I'm Lucille," the bartender called over. "But everyone calls me 'Lucky'." She squeezed a lime wedge into the glass, added seltzer with a flourish, then garnished with a sprig of mint. She obviously had strong hands—another weakness of mine. "And you are?"

"Niss. Well, I'm Janice, but it's such an old-fashioned name I started making everyone call me Niss when I was thirteen." I felt myself blushing. Being so directly and completely the focus of the other woman's attention was more intoxicating than the wine.

"Well, Niss..." Lucky paused, placed a straw in the glass, and then put it down in front of me. "This is the best virgin mojito I've ever made. I hope you enjoy it." She winked and went back to the other end of the bar where a waitress was waiting.

I watched Lucky for another moment. There was something liquid and graceful about the way she moved that made it almost impossible to look away. My imagination turned briefly impure, but I shook my head to clear my thoughts and pulled out my phone. I looked through the books I had downloaded and pulled the virgin mojito closer. Nothing on my phone caught my interest, so I flipped to my crossword app.

I finished the puzzle I'd started the night before as well as my drink. I was starting to feel a lot more myself. More sober at any rate. I flipped to the next puzzle and smiled when I realized the theme was mixology. Right as I was starting to read the first clue, a shadow blocked my light. I looked up and found Lucky.

"You aren't texting that guy in the glasses, are you? You know it's too soon. You're supposed to wait a couple days at least." Lucky's grin was cheeky, and it made me grin back.

"I was working on a crossword puzzle, but what do you know about the guy in the glasses?"

"I know that Dave and Kim come in here semi-regularly for dinner with that adorable daughter of theirs and that they've been conspiring to set the two of you up for a while." The bartender looked around then leaned closer. "If I'd known how beautiful you'd turn out to be, I'd've told them to set you up with me instead."

My mouth dropped open but I closed it quickly. "Do you always come on this strong?"

"Only when I've caught the beauty in question checking me out earlier in the evening." Lucky planted both of her elbows on the bar and rested her chin in her hands.

I pursed my lips for a moment, trying not to laugh. I looked away briefly, but finally I gave in. "And does it usually work?"

"Well, I'm cute and I'm a bartender. What do you think?" Lucky's voice had dropped in volume. It felt intimate, like how she'd talk in bed. I was definitely sparking with the redheaded bartender.

"I couldn't even begin to guess."

Lucky moved a little closer and I held my breath. We were almost close enough to kiss, and I realized I wanted that. I *really* wanted that. Then she stopped, close enough to touch but not actually touching.

I could smell mint on her breath. It smelled nice. She smelled nice. "To tell you the truth, I haven't been a bartender all that long and I've never tried this approach before, in or out of a bar. So, you really will have to tell me what you think. Is it working?"

"It's not *not* working."

Lucky's grin softened to something more real, something that reached her eyes. "You really are beautiful."

There was a clattering behind me, and it startled both of us. Lucky looked in the direction of the noise, nodded at whatever or whoever was there, and then met my eyes again. She blushed. "I forgot where we were."

"Me, too." I looked over my shoulder and took in the man standing there. He was staring at Lucky pointedly.

"I should go talk to him." Lucky shrugged one shoulder then left me alone again, moving out from behind the bar to talk with him.

I was surprised at myself. I hadn't reacted to someone this strongly since I was in my late twenties. At forty-five, I should have known better, but I found myself contemplating throwing caution to the wind and doing something I hadn't done since my early twenties. I wanted to take the bartender home with me.

When the voices behind me stopped, I expected Lucky to make her way behind the bar again, but I was surprised. She took the stool next to me and gave me a smirk. "My cousin told me to stop flirting with the customers."

"Cousin?"

"Yeah, uh," Lucky looked away then back. "My family owns this place."

"And you haven't been a bartender for long?" I wanted to know a little more about this woman. As attracted to her as I was, I knew I still needed to be cautious.

She shrugged. "Six months? Long, boring story. I'd rather talk about you."

"Oh?" I leaned towards Lucky. "Are you going to come on a bit too strong again? Or are you going to take seducing me seriously?" I didn't know where the boldness had come from, but I was going with it. It was probably the combination of a full year of full-time employment, wine, and an incredibly handsome woman.

Lucky sat back, her eyes wide. "What?"

It was my turn to sit back, startled. "Did I misread you? Were you just flirting with me for a better tip? If so, no worries. I'll tip well. Waited tables when I was younger and I know it's grueling work. I just..." I didn't know how to end that sentence. Had the wine gotten the better of me after all?

"No!" She laughed and I could have sworn it was musical. "I wasn't just flirting to get a better tip. Just that, well, I'm used to doing the chasing, not being chased."

"Oh." I leaned closer to her. "Is that a problem?"

"No, but what about Spectacles?" She stilled, a blush lighting up her cheeks.

I was feeling very bold indeed. "Are you really going to turn down an opportunity to come home with me tonight over the fact that I'm attracted to men as well?"

A shiver ran through Lucky. "No. I don't care if you're bi. Just that you two seemed to be getting along and I'd hate to get in the way, but if that's not an issue..." She swallowed loudly. Was she nervous? "You really want to take me home? Is that how it is?"

"If that's how you want it to be." I wanted to lean forward and kiss her, or at least run my hand up her thigh, but I restrained myself. I wanted this woman, but I'd content myself with fantasies if need be.

Her eyes went half-lidded and she leaned back before looking me up and down. "Yes, that's how I want it to be. But don't you have to work tomorrow?"

"Nope. I teach in the English department at Pittsford, just like Kim. Submitted grades earlier this evening, and the first summer session doesn't start for a couple of weeks. There are things I need to do, but nothing critical. I'm kind of on vacation." I held her gaze and realized that the eyes I'd taken for the typical green that so often accompanies red hair were actually flecked with gold.

"I'd prefer my place. That work for you?" She licked her bottom lip then bit it gently. I was going to spontaneously combust from wanting this woman.

I nodded then leaned forward. "Would I get you in trouble if I kissed you right now?"

Lucky let out a shuddering breath and drew back. "Yeah, you would. But don't worry. As luck would have it, Bear came to tell me that I should close a little early. Normally close this part of The Warren at 11:00 on weeknights, but it's slower than normal tonight."

I looked at my phone. It was 10:30. "Do I need to get out of your way? I can move to another part of The Warren."

Lucky stood from the stool, leaving her between my parted legs. From the grin she gave me, it wasn't by accident. "Probably a good idea. Not because you can't be here. But because you're so distracting. How about I meet you up near the front door?" She raked me up and down with her gaze. "Do you do this often? Dazzle poor, unsuspecting bartenders with your beauty then whisk them away to your bed?"

"Only when they're impossibly sexy redheads."

"All the time, then?" The grin Lucky gave me then wasn't seductive or even cheeky. It was filled with genuine amusement. I smiled back.

"Every time I've been to a bar in the last couple of years. Meaning just the once."

Lucky laughed, a low and rich sound. "I'll see you up front, Niss. I'm already mostly done shutting things down, so it won't be long."

"Wait," I said as I got down from the stool. "What do I owe you?"

"Kim and Dave paid for the wine and I got the virgin mojito. Now go." She made a shooing motion. "The sooner you let me finish, the sooner we can find a bed."

Chapter Two

I checked my email, then got engrossed in the new crossword puzzle again while I waited, so I didn't see Lucky approaching. Instead, I heard her voice close up, right behind me. "Shall we get out of here?"

I turned to face her. She was close enough to kiss, but I was suddenly conscious of the fact that her family owned The Warren and one or more of them were probably watching us. "Absolutely."

We'd made it outside and away from the door when Lucky stopped short in front of me. I only barely managed to not bump into her. "What?"

Lucky spun to face me, an oddly nervous expression on her face. She reached out, grabbed my hand, and pulled me into a shadow under some trees at the side of the building.

"What?" I asked again.

She didn't answer. Instead, she crowded me against the trunk of one of the trees. We were close in height, but Lucky was just a little bit taller, which forced me to lean my head back to look at her. Having all of her pressed up against all of me flooded my senses, but I was still confused.

"Lucky, what is it?"

"This," she finally answered before capturing my lips in a kiss. And what a kiss, unlike any I'd experienced before. From how strong she'd come onto me, I expected a brutal onslaught and welcomed the idea. That wasn't what I got. Instead, what happened was something more decadent and considered, the brush of slightly chapped lips against mine followed by her pressing my chin down with hers and then her tongue gently caressing mine. Everything else in the world faded away in the warmth of that kiss.

She pulled back and I tried to follow, to continue that magical connection, but she held me in place. Lucky looked at me with wonder in her eyes. "Wanted to make sure the chemistry was real, and damn, woman, that was... that was maybe the best first kiss of my life."

"Me, too." I felt breathless.

Lucky rested her forehead against mine. "I only live a mile and a half from here, and the weather was perfect this afternoon, so I walked. Are you good to drive? Because we shouldn't leave your car here after the place closes."

I nodded. "Last sip of wine was over an hour ago." I kissed her again, quick. "My car is this way."

We were quiet in the car, other than the few directions I needed to get from The Warren to Lucky's home, but the car felt filled with everything as yet unspoken. The urge to touch and be touched, the desire for skin against skin, the need to taste every part of this woman beside me. I almost couldn't breathe with how much I ached for her.

She directed me to a driveway that led to tiny bungalow tucked behind a bigger house and had me park. A light came on, startling me, and she smiled reassuringly. "Don't worry. Motion sensors. My father's out of town."

"Your father?" I looked around the backyard again.

"I don't live with him," she rushed to tell me. "Just in his guest house."

I shot her a quick smile. "I lived with my parents in my late thirties for a little while. I wouldn't judge."

Lucky looked at me intently then surged over the armrest to capture my lips in an intense kiss. When we came up for air, she laughed. "I suppose we should move this inside."

Once we were in her home, Lucky didn't even bother to turn any lights on before she pounced again. She pushed me up against the front door, hard, and kissed me breathless. She made me tingle and thrum. Her lips slid from mine, down my chin, and along my throat. "You okay with this coming off?" She tugged at the bottom hem of my T-shirt.

"God, yes," I answered before doing the honors myself.

There wasn't a lot of available light, but still Lucky looked at me reverentially. "So sexy. So fucking sexy." She grabbed my hand and pulled me down a hall to a bedroom. "Didn't make my bed this morning. Didn't know I'd have a goddamn goddess here tonight, so I hope you'll forgive me."

We tumbled onto that unmade bed and I couldn't help laughing. The laugh was cut off when she pushed me onto my back and lowered her mouth to the valley between my breasts. "Anything you don't like? Places I shouldn't touch?" The words were muffled.

"I don't know. No?" Lucky bit my nipple gently through my bra. "It's been a while, almost a year, so I'm up for almost anything." I arched my back, pushing my breast into her mouth, wanting more touch, more contact.

Suddenly, she moved her mouth away. I whimpered in protest but she scooted up anyway. Lucky cupped my cheek and looked down at me. I couldn't read her expression with so little light. "It's been a while for me, too. Couple of years."

I took advantage of her stillness to start undoing the buttons of her shirt. "I'm not very feminine." Her voice sounded smaller, apprehensive.

"If you'd rather I not?" I stopped unbuttoning and looked up into a face I couldn't quite see. I wanted her naked, but that didn't mean I could demand it.

"Just don't want you to be disappointed."

"Are you disappointed? I'm not skinny, after all."

"No! I love a woman with curves."

"And I love women with muscles." I looked at her pointedly.

Lucky sat up and pulled her shirt over her head, and the little bit of light caught a toned yet feminine torso. I reached up a hand as she pulled off a sports bra, and I whimpered. I couldn't believe I was getting to touch this woman.

"I got tested the last time I saw my gynecologist. About four months ago. All clear." I sat up enough to be able to reach behind me and unfastened my own bra.

The woman lying halfway on me groaned. "God, Niss. Just look at you." She reached over and flicked on the lamp beside her bed. "There, that's better."

I posed with my back arched then winked at her. "When was the last time you were tested?"

"Hmm?" Lucky seemed like she was trying to touch me everywhere at once and I broke her concentration.

"I asked," I said as I gently pushed her over and onto her back, "when you were last tested, because I'm hoping to spend a good amount of time between your thighs and I don't have a dental dam on me." I kissed down her neck, flicked each of her nipples once with the tip of my tongue, then kissed further down her torso. In the soft glow of lamp light, I could see that the freckles did indeed extend this far down.

"Fuck, that feels good." Lucky shivered. "About eight months ago. All good."

"Good to hear." I moved back up and took one of her nipples into my mouth while I fumbled with her belt.

Clothes slowly came off, and every inch revealed demanded to be caressed, nipped, licked. Her skin tasted amazing, a bit salty from sweat but under that was something else—probably a soap or a lotion. It was intoxicating.

Lucky seemed as intent on tasting and touching every bit of me, until eventually there was nothing in the way. I pulled back for a moment so I could see exactly who I was in bed with. Lucky was glorious. There were freckles everywhere. Everywhere. Except where the complicated Celtic-styled tattoo sleeve traveled up her left arm and culminated in a wolf's head biting at her collar bone. She had the toned body of someone whose strength is part of their job, but she wasn't cut. Her small breasts were high and firm, which I already knew, and her skin was flawless. I looked further down and found a thick thatch of tight curls at the juncture of her legs that was a shade or two darker than the hair atop her head. I couldn't believe *this* woman wanted me. I wasn't going to waste this opportunity.

When my eyes rose again to her face, I was thrilled to see the heat there was undiminished.

"Wow, Niss. You really are made up of nothing but curves." Her eyes roamed over my body, making my skin feel even more heated.

"Come here," I told her.

She flung herself into my arms and immediately took control of me with another commanding kiss. Her thigh nudged mine apart and she groaned as she made contact with my already wet pussy. We kissed like we were each dying of thirst and the other was a glass of cool water, hands roaming frantically as we ground against each other.

Eventually, I remembered my plan and pushed her onto her back. "Been wanting to do this since I first walked into your bar and saw you."

I traced my tongue along the wolf's head then pulled back. As much as I wanted to taste every inch of her ink, I had other things to do. I kissed my way down her torso and wedged her thighs apart before lying down across the bed.

Lucky started quivering as I hooked her thighs over my shoulders. I looked up at her. "You okay with this?"

She stared at me then nodded. I saw her lips part, and it looked like she formed the word 'please,' but there was no sound.

The power I held over her was heady. I wrapped my arms around her thighs and watched her. Lucky started to squirm. She was so aroused I could smell it.

"Niss," she begged, so I gave in. Parting her hair, I gave one long lick with the tip of my tongue from bottom to top.

A sigh of pure bliss escaped Lucky and I couldn't help smiling. Not only was I getting to touch this woman, but I was also getting to bring her joy. Heady indeed.

"Do you like fingers, too? Or just my mouth?" I teased her clit with a flicker of my tongue. Couldn't resist.

"Whatever you want, just touch me. Can't remember last time I was this turned on. Please. *Please.*" This was all a whimper. I watched her face, contorted with pleasure and desperation.

"Sexiest thing I've ever seen," I told her, then went to work. I started gently, with just my lips and tongue, testing her responses and relishing every quiver, every moan, and every gasp. Her hands came down to tangle in my hair, holding me in place.

Lucky tried to raise her hips to grind against my mouth but I pushed her back down. "Told you I've been wanting to do this since I first set eyes on you. What part of that makes you think I wanted to rush and give you a merely adequate orgasm?"

She looked down at me, eyes wild. She opened her mouth as if to say something but I didn't really want an answer, so I started to torment her again. I sucked on her clit, insistently, and all that came out of Lucky's mouth was a loud moan.

I felt her thighs start to quiver and gave up teasing her. I focused all my effort on repeating the exact motion that made her shake, then did it again and again. I thought about how I could lose myself in this woman. She was sex personified, and I was painfully turned on just from giving her head.

"Please," Lucky whispered. "Please please please."

I didn't know what she was asking for, but I wasn't going to stop. I thought she had to be close, and now I needed her orgasm as badly as she did. When she raised her hips again, I let her. I let this delicious woman use me and did my best to keep up with the rhythm she set. Lucky's grip on my hair became painful. Her heels dug into my back, and she called my name out loudly as the taste of her got sweeter. Her whole body seemed to shake, almost violently, but then she froze and said my name once more, this time a whisper.

We stayed like that for long enough that my shoulders started to hurt, but Lucky relaxed before I could think to complain.

"Holy..." Lucky breathed the word as she let go of my hair.

I rested my cheek against her thigh and wiped my face off. "Yeah?"

She laughed. "Holy shit, Niss. Holy shit."

"Am I right to take that as a compliment?" I was fishing, no two ways about it.

"Yes, a compliment." She sat up and cupped my cheek. "I couldn't tell you the last time I came that hard."

"Good." I grinned up at her.

"Come here," she said and pulled me so I was lying next to her. "You're amazing."

I laughed.

"No, I mean it." Lucky leaned forward and kissed me gently. "Thought it would be a boring Monday night like any other." She stroked firmly down my side, a touch that sent tremors through me. "End up having astonishing sex with one of the most beautiful women I've ever seen."

I let the compliment wash over me without reacting. I was too horny to really think about it, anyway. I grabbed her hand and put it where I needed it. I parted my thighs to let her have better access.

"That's what you want?" She asked, teasing her finger all around without actually touching.

"Yes. I have a thing about hands. You have good hands," I told her, squirming. I was seconds from begging. "Strong hands."

I worried for nothing. Lucky teased my labia for a moment and we both groaned as she pushed two fingers inside me.

"All that from going down on me?" She murmured as she crooked her fingers to touch that sensitive ridge of flesh inside me. It felt like lightning winging through my veins.

"Yes, oh oh oh, yes, just like that."

Lucky had twisted her hand so that her thumb was rubbing my clit even as her fingers moved inside me. I looked up at her, and when our eyes met, the connection between us seemed to sharpen.

"Want to see you come. *Need* to see you come." She kissed me, hard, then pulled her head back. "Come for me, Niss. Come now."

"Can't come on demand," I gasped, "but don't worry—I'm close. So close. So close."

Lucky leaned down and took one of my nipples into her mouth. God, it felt good. Everything she did to me felt good and my body was on fire. Her fingers inside, her thumb on me, and her mouth, all driving me closer and closer to the edge. Then the bright ball that had been gathering inside of me finally burst into a billion pieces and I shuddered, my entire body so tense I thought I might sprain something. It went on and on, good and great and amazing, and when every drop of possible pleasure had been wrung out of me, I collapsed back onto the bed.

"Wonderful. Utterly and completely wonderful." Lucky murmured these words against my temple. She gently pulled her hand away and then wiped it clean on the sports bra she'd worn earlier. My companion gathered me closer, tangled her legs with mine, and let out a contented sigh. Then she suddenly tensed up. "I'm a cuddler. Is that okay?"

I laughed. "As hard as you just made me come? You could probably perform minor surgery on me and I wouldn't mind." I twisted my head to look at her. "But cuddling is great, regardless."

"Good," she said, but her voice was small. Still, her arms tightened around me. "Been kinda lonely since I moved here. Lots of family, but I didn't really know most of them before. Not well, anyway."

I hummed in sympathy and stroked her back.

"Up until recently, I've been too busy focusing on work to think about being lonely," I told her. "I do have some friends, but time to see them has been scarce. I grew up here. Moved away for college. Came back about ten years ago. I could look up my old friends, I'm sure, but—like I said—busy. So, I know the feeling."

We lay like that for a while. The tingle of skin on skin was still there, and I thought about how I could get used to that.

"Hey, do you like ice cream?" Lucky spoke against my chest, so the words were muffled.

"Yes. Why do you ask?"

She pulled away and grinned at me. "Want some mint chocolate chip?"

I grinned back. "Love some."

She returned with a tub of ice cream and two spoons. What could I do other than sit there, completely naked, completely sated, sharing mint chocolate chip ice cream with her? It was decadent and surreal and lovely. Also, romantic. We didn't speak for a few minutes, just ate ice cream and giggled like we were teenagers.

I studied Lucky. She caught me looking and grinned. "What?"

"I just can't imagine you lacking for company is all." I shrugged.

"Despite my nickname, I'm not all that lucky in relationships." She held my gaze and then looked away. "I used to have lots of friends. I was an OR nurse back in New Hampshire. Worked mostly with cardiac surgeons. It's hard not to make friends when you're dealing with life and death that way. Even dated one of those surgeons for a couple of years." She sighed. "But then my stepdad died suddenly and a couple of months later my mother was diagnosed with liver cancer. I ended up quitting my job to take care of her. She died a year after he did. Got out of the habit of making friends, and the ones I had all kind of, I dunno, drifted away."

"Oh" was all I could think of to say.

Finally, her eyes swung around to me again. "I could say the same to you about being alone."

"I had to work three jobs to make ends meet for a long, long time. And even that was an improvement over living in my parents' basement like I did my first couple of years back in Rochester. Finally, I have just one job, but first year in a tenure-track job is a lot." I shrugged. "Self-inflicted wound, though, since I'm the fool who wanted a PhD and to teach at the college level."

"Beautiful *and* smart." Lucky grinned.

"How smart is it really to go into all that debt for a job that doesn't actually pay that well?" I laughed.

"Don't do that. A PhD is nothing to sneeze at. Besides, if nothing else, you were smart to come home with me tonight." Her grin grew broader. She reached out for the spoon I'd been holding. "Be right back."

Lucky disappeared down the hall and I looked around for my clothes. As fun and romantic as this had been, I was the random customer she brought home for sex. That was over and I wanted to get out before it turned awkward. I finally spotted my underwear and started to put my clothes back on.

"You're getting dressed?"

I spun around and found Lucky standing in the doorway.

"Um, yeah." I pulled my underwear all the way up. "I went home with the sexy bartender to have hot sex and, well, we did that."

"Sexy, huh?" She grinned.

"Obviously," I told her, rolling my eyes. "Do you know where my bra went to?"

"It's just," she said, closing the distance between us, "big as that orgasm you gave me was, it barely took the edge off. I got really revved up watching you. Do you know you bite your lip when you're concentrating? You did it in the bar, too. I imagined it was when you came to a crossword puzzle clue that stumped you. I kept thinking how I wanted to be the one biting your lip." She cupped my chin and then did just that. "Spent the last part of my shift turned on and wanting you."

"What are you saying?" I couldn't help myself; I ran my hands up her back and over her muscled shoulders. She shivered nicely at my touch.

"I'm saying I'd like a second round before you go." Lucky licked along my lower lip. "I'd love to get you on your hands and knees and fuck you with my strap-on. Maybe smack that juicy ass of yours a couple of times while I'm at it, if you'd be open to that. Didn't really get to explore all these curves earlier in my race to get you off."

It was my turn to shiver.

"Stay a little longer?" She put her arms around me and tucked her fingertips just inside my panties. "Let me make you come again?"

"What an invitation, just..." I stopped because Lucky was drawing my underwear back down. The sight of her kneeling in front of me was intoxicating.

"Just?" She looked up. The woman knew exactly what she was doing to me.

"Just, when it's time for me to go—really time for me to go—please don't be awkward about it. Tell me you need to get some sleep or something like that, and I'll be gone. Deal?"

She kissed the swell of my belly quickly then stood up again. "Deal. Now"—Lucky bumped against me and pushed me back towards her bed—"enough talk. I want to fuck you again."

Chapter Three

I opened my eyes and was surprised to find myself somewhere other than my own bed. It only took me a couple of seconds to remember going out with friends and then home with the sexy bartender. The last was brought home by the fact that I was obviously using a tattooed arm as a pillow. I snuggled into her embrace. Waking up in someone's arms was a delight I hadn't experienced in a while.

Memories came back quickly then—of being fucked so hard I thought I'd walk funny today and coming even harder, of Lucky asking for one more cuddle, and of telling her that I should go because I was getting sleepy. But nothing after that.

I looked around and realized things did not match my memories. Last night, this was a normal, if small, bedroom. I remembered a dresser with a scattering of small objects on the top, a couple of bedside tables with lamps and a half-drunk glass of water, and a sweet reproduction of Andrew Wyeth's painting, *Master Bedroom*. Now, everything I looked at seemed to be covered in varying amounts of gold. I knew I wasn't drunk when I got here. I wouldn't have driven if I'd been even a little tipsy. I knew everything in here had been normal.

I would have noticed glistening gold, even distracted as I was by some of the best sex of my life. What was going on?

I turned over and found that Lucky was still sleeping peacefully. She looked different, too. Lucky was still Lucky, red hair with a strip of white and plump, kissable lips. But her nose was more pointed and her eyebrows were bushier and her ears... Her ears were incredibly pointed. Like a Vulcan or an elf. Was this a practical joke she was playing on me for falling asleep here? It all looked too real to have been done as a joke and, besides, the set up would have woken me.

"Lucky?" I called softly. I was feeling a little frantic, but I didn't see a need to be rude. Not yet, anyway. At least that's what I told my impending panic attack.

"Hmm?" Without opening her eyes, she snuggled closer to me and let out a contented sigh, but then went still. Her eyes popped open and I noticed they were way greener than any human eyes ever were, bright emerald. A look of horror was on her face. "You're still here. Why are you still here?"

"I told you I was getting sleepy. You told me five more minutes. That's the last thing I remember. Are we really going to talk about the fact that I fell asleep while being cuddled? Or are we, I dunno, *going to talk about the gold?*" I was losing my cool. I could feel it seeping away. I thought about how, where we were, nobody would hear my scream. If this woman who had flung me around the bed during our second round decided to hurt me, I was fucked. And not in a good way. I was also very aware of the fact that she was still holding me. I could feel fear creeping up, but I fought it.

Lucky started breathing fast and her eyes got enormous. "You weren't supposed the see the gold. Aren't supposed to see the gold."

I tried to pull away from her, but she whimpered and held on.

"What about me? Do I look different?" Her voice was very low. Last night, that resonance had thrilled me. This morning it was scaring me.

"If I say no, will you let go of me?"

Lucky closed her eyes and cursed under her breath.

"How about if I promise not to say anything to anyone? Ever. Nobody would believe me anyway." I took in a breath, trying to calm down, but it didn't work. "Please, just let me go. I'll forget we ever met."

Her eyes popped open again. She looked regretful. Somehow, that scared me more. I was in danger. "Can't just take your word for it. Going to have to make you forget, for real. I don't have the magic for it, but one of my cousins might. I don't know." Lucky sighed as she finally let go of me. She swung her legs over the side of the bed and stared at the wall. "Fuck. I really liked you, too. Was going to ask for your phone number and if I could see you again. And now I'm going to have to make you forget. This is just like Nia all over again. How have I not gotten better at this since I was fifteen?"

"Magic?" I asked, but then I thought about it. Red hair. Bushy eyebrows. Gold. Alcohol. I knew I should try to run, but I had to ask, "You're a little tall, and obviously female, but are you a clurichaun?"

Lucky twisted around to face me, shocked. "No. A leprechaun. Well, half. And the height myth was based on one specific family in Ireland. Most of us are human sized."

"Are clurichauns real, too? Or the Tuatha De Danann? Banshees?" My love of myths and legends and my curiosity were overpowering my sense of self-preservation, but opportunities like this never fell in my lap. "What about dullahans? The headless horsemen? If those are real, maybe Washington Irving saw one and worked it into 'The Legend of Sleepy Hollow'."

"I don't know which are real. I've never even heard of tua... tuath..."

"Tuatha De Danann. It means 'the folk of the goddess Danu.' They were most famously depicted in John Duncan's painting *Riders of the Sidhe*. Pre-Christian, Irish deities." I let the blanket slip in my excitement, but when Lucky glanced down, I pulled it back up.

"How do you know all this?"

"I teach English at Pittsford College, but I'm a folklorist. I did my dissertation in comparative folklore with a focus on the distinctions between the literature of European stories and the way they've evolved in the United States." I pulled the blanket further, all the way up to my chin. "I know folklore."

She sighed again, her whole body seeming to deflate. "You're even more perfect than I thought. Of course I have to make you forget me. Just my luck. I can give it to others, but never myself. This is going to be worse than Nia."

"Look, I hate to interrupt, but I do need to use the bathroom." I thought that maybe I could sneak out a window. I told myself to be calm. To breathe normally. I couldn't give myself away. "Can you give me a moment of privacy to get dressed and then remind me where the bathroom is?"

"First door on the right out of the bedroom."

I looked around. "My clothes?"

There was a flash of something, maybe pain or regret, on Lucky's face, but it was quickly gone. "I'll turn my back. Your clothes are on the floor at the foot of the bed."

She turned to face the wall, giving me an uncomfortable view of her still naked form.

I dressed quickly.

"Just so you know, the window in the bathroom is too small to climb out."

When I was finished using the bathroom, I turned to the window and studied it. It was indeed small. It opened, and the whole opening was maybe two feet square, but the window itself was one of those side to side double glazed windows that were so popular for bathrooms. If I'd still been a child, I might have been able to fit through, but there was no way I would now.

My panic rose again, so I sat on the edge of the tub, trying to breathe normally. When I'd finally managed it, I returned to the bedroom and found my erstwhile lover dressed and on the phone.

My mind raced with a dozen half-formed escape plans, but I also wanted to hear what she was saying.

"I know you can't, but can you just come over?" Lucky noticed me, started to smile, but then remembered herself. "Yes. Please." She listened for a little longer. "Uh huh. Okay. See you soon." She hung up.

"Um, are you hungry? I'm not the greatest of breakfast cooks, but I can do scrambled eggs and toast. And I've got coffee. Tea, too, if you'd prefer that." Lucky sounded nervous. "Unless you have dietary restrictions? Not like that kind of thing came up in conversation last night."

"What would happen if I just left?" She had my purse at her feet, which held my car keys, but I could walk. I could run. "Just turned around and walked out the front door and away?"

"I'd have to stop you," she said, plain as day. "I wouldn't hurt you on purpose, but I can't let you leave." She shook her head rapidly. "Besides, this will probably be over soon. My cousin and his mother should be here any minute. My cousin can't do memory magic, but his mom can. While we're waiting, let me make you some breakfast."

I crossed my arms over my chest. "Not hungry. Something about being afraid I'll be hurt because I picked the wrong bartender to go home with took my appetite." My fear had shifted to anger, and I wasn't going to hold back.

Lucky winced, then sighed. "You just felt so good in my arms. I didn't want to let go."

"And now I have to pay the price." I looked around the room, which was once again normal. Lucky herself also looked like she had when we met the previous evening. I gestured to the space. "The cat's out of the bag, why hide it now?"

She finally put her phone in her pocket and stood. "Thought it might make you feel more comfortable to have everything look like this. I fucked up and... I realized I haven't said this yet, but I'm sorry. Like you said, this was my mistake and you're the one who's going to have to pay for it. But, please, let me at least make you some coffee."

I let out a sigh. Somehow, Lucky being kind in the face of my ire made me feel like I was kicking a puppy. "I drink tea in the morning, but what I'd really like is to brush my teeth. I looked around your bathroom, but I didn't find a spare toothbrush. Do you have one?"

Lucky nodded. "Linen closet in the hall. Here, let me get it for you." She moved past me, but stopped. She turned to look at me then at something behind me. "I'm just going to..." I watched, speechless, as she dug in my purse and pulled out my phone and my keys. She put both in the pocket of her hoodie, and went back to the hall. When she returned with an unopened toothbrush, I snatched it and went back to the bathroom. I did the best I could with what was there, brushing my teeth and washing my face, but I still felt gross when I once again emerged from the bathroom.

"Who's Nia?" I asked when I found her still in her bedroom.

If I didn't know better, I'd think she looked haunted. "This girl I liked in high school. We were friends, but I wanted more. When I found out about being a leprechaun, I told her then I confessed about my feelings. She said she liked me, too, but my father found out I'd told our secret and erased Nia's memories." She sighed.

There was a knock at the front door, and then it opened. Lucky squeezed past me in the narrow hall. "Sorry," she muttered.

"My Bear tells me you've got yourself in a pickle, but he wouldn't tell me the rest. Said it was your tale, not his. What's the trouble, Lucille my girl?" I followed the voices to the living room and found a tall, skinny man who was probably a few years younger than me. He had dark auburn hair and was leaning against the wall. There was also a short, older but still vibrant woman with the same color hair threaded through with silver and twisted back into a bun. The family resemblance, especially their chins and their green eyes, was unmistakable.

"Ah, who's this?" The woman asked.

Everyone's eyes turned to me. "I'm Niss and I'm the pickle. Nice to meet you." I did nothing to hide the anger from my voice.

"I, um, brought her home last night and we fell asleep before I could ask her to go home or refresh the illusion spells. When we woke, she saw..." Lucky started, but the woman interrupted her.

"She saw your gold and your true shape, I'm guessing." Then she laughed, loud and long. "We've all been there, Lucky. Have I ever told you about the time I had to have my brother, your da, perform memory magic on Carlos Santana at Woodstock? Your da was so talented that he actually convinced Carlos he'd been hallucinating on mescaline most of the day."

"Really?" Lucky seemed enchanted by what her aunt had done. I was disgusted.

"Hello, Niss, I'm Bearach Murphy. Lucky's cousin. And this person doing her best to embarrass me is my mother, Shannon Murphy."

The tall man crossed to me and put his hand out for me to shake. I recognized him from the bar the previous night.

I kept my arms crossed over my chest and looked at his hand. "Your cousin asked you here to erase my memories, so you'll forgive me if I'm not feeling overly cordial."

I was going to ride the anger as long as I could. Sure, it was really fear masquerading as outrage, but it was better than cowering in a corner—which felt like my only other option.

"It's been since last night, you say?" Shannon crossed to me as well.

"Well, only since we woke this morning." Lucky looked over at me then away. I hoped she felt as awful as it seemed. "So... a little over an hour."

"Beyond my talents, then. I can do five minutes easy. An hour if I'm prepared and really rested. But I've spent my energy in other ways, not honing my 'chaun skills." She looked over at me. "We all live a mostly human existence. Despite what tales you might have heard." She shook her head. "No, for this we'll need your da."

"Then get him. Right away. I have things to do." I looked each of my audience members in the face. "I just want to get out of here."

Lucky winced audibly. "Ouch."

"Can't. He's out of town," Bear said.

"Remember? I told you last night," Lucky added.

"Then call him up and ask him to come home early. Tell him you need his help right away. I have a life and I really shouldn't have to pay this steep a price for a momentary lapse in judgement." I could feel the dread rising again.

"My dear... what did you say your name is?" Shannon took a step towards me, but I stepped back, maintaining the distance between us.

"I'm Janice but I go by Niss."

"My dear Janice, then. Lovely name, by the way. Why don't you go by your full name? I used to know a Janis decades ago. Of course, she probably spelled it differently from you." Shannon looked at me consideringly but not unkindly. "Poor thing died young. I still sometimes wonder what kind of music she would have made later in her life if she'd lived."

"Mam," Bear groaned and rolled his eyes.

"Ah, yes. As I was saying, my dear Janice, my brother isn't just out of town, he's unreachable. So, we can't just tell him we need his help. We can't tell him anything." At least she had the good grace to look embarrassed.

"Then what are we going to do about this?" I gestured for Bear and Shannon to get out of my way so I could get to Lucky. "You said this was your fuck-up. You said you were sorry. You said this would be fixed."

She plopped down on the couch and refused to meet my eyes. "I really thought Aunt Shannon would be able to."

"Well, what are we going to do about this?" I spun on the rest of her family. "She's obviously useless. How are the two of you going to help? Or, might I suggest, you all could let me go and take my word that I won't speak of this to anyone. I mean, do you think anyone would believe me if I said one of the bartenders at The Warren is really a leprechaun and, by the way, she made me *come so hard I saw stars*?" I was shouting now, but I didn't care. I also didn't care that I'd just confessed to Lucky's family how good the sex was. I just wanted out of there. "Where is my purse, Lucky? Did you leave it in the bedroom?" I went charging down the hall and found my purse was indeed still in the bedroom. I grabbed it and turned to the window to see if I could open it. I had a spare car key in my wallet and my parents had spare keys to my apartment. I would worry about my work keys later.

"I can't let you do that." Bear pulled me back from the window, gently at first but then more firmly. "Trusting humans not to tell is how people learned of our existence in the first place. Leprechauns and others like us take that very seriously." I tried to fight him, but Bear put his arms around me and held me still. "Please, Niss, don't resist. We'll get it fixed for you. It just might take some time."

I shrugged his arms away and sat on the bed.

"You're holding me prisoner and asking me not to make a fuss about it. You see the problem there, right?" How could this room that had been the scene of some of the best sex of my life now be my prison?

"Look," Bear said, sitting next to me, "I'm friends with a satyr who could probably help. I'm going to call him and see if he will come over. If he can't, maybe he knows someone who can. And if worst comes to worst, Uncle Brian is supposed to be back in six days and we will make sure you're as comfortable as possible in the meantime."

I finally met his eyes. "I wish you could trust me enough to know that I really wouldn't tell."

Bear nodded. "I wish I knew you well enough to know whether or not I could trust you."

I shrugged.

The man leaned closer and lowered his voice. "Listen, is my cousin really that good in bed?"

The laugh that came out of me then startled us both.

His mother found us like that, laughing. "Bear, you stay here and keep Janice company. Make her some breakfast, too. I'm going to look around Brian's house for things to make her more comfortable while she has to stay here."

"I was going to call Leander."

"That's a good idea, my boy." Shannon smiled down at both of us. "And Janice, my dear, I sent Lucille to your apartment for clothes and toiletries and such. Can't have you sitting around in that outfit for a week, just in case that nice satyr boy can't help. Is there any medicine or anything else she should pick up while she's there?"

All at once, a sense of doom settled over me, and I the panic attack I'd been keeping at bay finally started. Even the thought of satyrs also being real wasn't enough to calm me. I stood and looked around, trying to find a way to escape.

"Mam, Leander is older than you and me and Brian put together. Older by a lot. He once let it slip that he's older than some of the gods we all know from Greek and Roman mythology." Bear was laughing, but it sounded like it was coming from a long way off. "You can't just call him a boy."

"He makes himself look young, so why not?" Shannon laughed with her son, then turned back to me. "Now, dear, have you thought of what I should ask Lucille... oh, no. You don't look well. Bearach, help Janice to sit. I'm going to get an ice pack."

I felt gentle hands guide me down the hall and back to the living room. I plopped down on Lucky's overstuffed couch and tried, to no real avail, to slow my breathing.

"Here, lean forward," Shannon urged me softly. When I did as she'd asked, I felt something blessedly cool come to rest against my neck. "I thought this might happen, but when you got angry, I hoped you were past it."

"Do I really need to stay here?" I asked when my breathing slowed enough that I could talk.

"Lucky asked the same thing, and the answer is yes. I told her she had to clean up her own mess. And this is probably the safest place for you. It's a little remote, so if you do something foolish like try to scream for help nobody will hear you."

"Fine," I said, then sat up and looked between my two captors. "There are some books on my desk." Maybe I could use this week to be productive.

"I'll let her know." Shannon tossed the cold pack to her son. "I'm going to put a warding spell up so you can't leave but won't have to stay in the house the whole time. And I'm going to see if my brother has an air mattress that Lucky can sleep on so you can have the bed. If nothing else, I think her couch might be a pull-out." She patted my knee. "We'll get you through this, and before you know it, you'll forget all about your time with us."

"If I'm just going to forget, don't worry about the books. I need to read them for an article I'm writing and it won't do me any good to read then forget." I couldn't help the sigh that came out. I needed to take some time off, really off, and had for a while, but I wasn't happy about it being forced on me. "Wait, how does she know where I live?"

"What?" Shannon tilted her head in confusion.

"How does Lucky know where I live so she can get my things? I know she took my keys, but how does she know where to go?" The panic was coming back. I could hear it in my voice and feel it in my bones.

"You had a piece of mail in your purse, love." She studied me. "Do we need to put your head between your knees again, or do you think you can breathe like a normal person?"

That made me laugh, which helped the panic subside. "What would you know about normal people? You're not even human!"

Shannon raised an eyebrow at me and I relented.

I let out a sigh. "I believe there was talk of breakfast?"

"That a girl, Janice. And you're in luck. He's a good cook, my Bear. Runs the kitchen at The Warren. Almost all the family works there." Shannon patted my knee again and then got up. "I'm truly sorry for this. First time I've seen Lucille interested in anyone since she moved here and it turns out like this. She's a good girl, I swear, just new to this life. Except the personal illusion—she's always had to do that since she turned fifteen. You must be as good in bed as you claim she is, to make her forget. Even if this is turning out poorly, I'm still glad she got some touch."

I opened my mouth to respond, unsure what I was going to say, but she'd left the room before I could think of anything. I still felt myself blushing.

"Imagine growing up with her as your mother." Bear got up.

"What are you going to do if my parents need me? They live in Webster, so they do sometimes call me for things with no warning." It rarely happened, even when they were home. They'd told me I was being silly to move back to Rochester just because they'd retired ten years prior, and they did still seem to be able to take care of themselves just fine, but I wasn't going to tell Bear that. I definitely wasn't going to tell him that they were on a two-week cruise on the Danube and had just left the previous Friday.

"We'll cross that bridge when we come to it, I guess. Now, how do you like your eggs?"

Chapter Four

I was arguing with Shannon and Bear about who was going to wash the dishes when the front door opened again. We all stood still and looked at each other, then Shannon called out, "Lucille, tell Janice that she's not to wash the dishes."

"What?" Lucky appeared in the kitchen door. She had my favorite duffle bag over one shoulder and a huge, reusable shopping bag from a local grocery store over the other. "Niss, you don't have to wash dishes."

I sucked in a breath. Hearing her say my name reminded me that the last time she'd said it, she was coming. I hated this so much, most of all because my body reacted to that carnal memory in the expected way.

"Fine. I won't. Far be it from me to be nice to your relatives who've been taking care of me in your absence." I charged up to her, grabbed my duffel, and headed to the living room. "And I'm taking the couch. If you'll do your best to stay out of that room while I'm forced to be here, that would be great."

I heard footsteps behind me and spun. It was Lucky.

"You *wanted* to wash the dishes?" Lucky stared at me, her expression a mix of shock and a goofy grin.

"They cooked for me, so I tried to help. I wanted to be nice to the people who are helping you with your fuck-up." I'd calmed down while Lucky was out of the house, but now my anger was back and had ramped up another dozen levels. I wasn't sure whether to blame this on unexpectedly still wanting her or on her kind and guileless face. Blame whatever. I was pissed.

"Really, I'll take the couch. That will make it easier for me to stay out of your way as much as possible. And I'm working a lot this week, so that will help. You should have the bed." I'd wiped the grin off Lucky's face. In fact, it looked like she might cry. I wasn't sure how to feel about that, but I told the initial surge of guilt to get lost.

"You're only working tonight, my girl. We covered your shifts for the rest of the week." Shannon came up behind Lucky and looped her arm around her niece's waist. "Janice might be an unwilling guest, but she's your guest. You won't leave her unattended, no matter how awkward it will be."

Lucky opened her mouth but then closed it again so quickly I heard her teeth click.

"If I'm sleeping in your bed, I want clean sheets." My pronouncement brought their eyes back to me.

"I can do that." Lucky put the shopping bag down on the coffee table. "That's for you, too." She disappeared down the hall to the bedroom.

"She's a sweet one. You're entitled to kick her around for what she's done to you, but I'd appreciate it if you try not to kick too hard." Shannon studied me.

"I'm angry. I can't help but be angry. You all are keeping me here against my wishes. I'm allowed to be angry, Shannon." In truth, I understood their need for secrecy. And I was warming up to Shannon and Bear. But this was a shitty situation, and I wasn't going to pretend otherwise just because I liked Lucky's relatives. Then I remembered that this would all be erased from my brain by the following week, so it was all for nothing anyway. And I felt deflated.

"You absolutely are allowed to be angry, but I'm fond of her. All my other brothers just gave me nephews. My girl, Aoife, and that girl are it for women in that generation in this family." She sighed. "Okay, Bear's going to leave with me shortly but he'll come back in a little bit. He'll be hanging around here in case you need anything. I can have him stay at the main house if you'd prefer, but I don't want to leave you alone. Meanwhile, can you come outside with me?"

I had just started to look through what Lucky had brought for me, so Shannon's request caught me off guard. "What? Why?"

"I need to test the barrier I put up," she said. "It was a fiddly bit of magic, letting you go outside but only so far. Always had a talent for boundary magic, but it's been some time. We need to test it." Shannon started to loop her arm through mine, but I pulled back. The older woman actually had the nerve to look a little hurt.

Lucky returned then. "She doesn't have to do anything she doesn't want to do, Aunt Shannon." Lucky was very adamant. "I mean, other than stay here until we can deal with my mistake."

I turned to face my erstwhile lover, but she was looking down and a light blush was creeping up her cheeks. I had a flash of wanting to thank her, but pushed the impulse away.

"We have to test to be sure, Lucille. Unless you're volunteering to never sleep between here and when we can get someone to help clean up your mess." Shannon was stern.

Finally, Lucky met my eyes. Her voice was low, apologetic. "If your head starts to hurt and you feel sick, stop where you are. Shannon's barriers usually make humans faint."

"Tsk. I would have warned her."

Shannon and I went outside, accompanied by Bear and Lucky, and tested the barrier.

There was a path around behind the house, through a wooded area, and we walked slowly along it. At regular intervals, Shannon asked me to step off the path away from the house. The one time I did more than test, trying to get away—not running, but going farther than I should have—I felt immediately dizzy and nauseated. I fought to keep my feet under me, and Lucky was instantly at my side holding me up. Once my head cleared, I pushed her away and rejoined Shannon without saying a word. By the time we'd made a full circuit, I knew my bounds. I was also a lot calmer. Sunshine had helped.

Other than the woods, there was a small and shaded seating area that I thought I'd make a lot of use of, but nothing else of note. I wondered if I'd get sick of it by the end of the week.

We had a brief discussion about my car—did it have one of those driver assist calling things installed, no; should we move it, no—and then it was time for Shannon and Bear to leave. They assured me that Bear would be back before Lucky had to leave for her shift at The Warren, then they got in a car and made a quick retreat.

"So, um, I..." Lucky started, but I turned and glared at her. She stumbled over her words until she finally started up again. "I don't know if you have any dietary restrictions or what you even like to eat, other than mint chocolate chip ice cream, and you're stuck here for a week. I can have Bear bring you something from The Warren, but beyond that is there anything you want? Don't like?"

She was being considerate, and it grated on my nerves. I wanted her to be rude. I wanted her to be dismissive. I wanted to hate her, really. But she wasn't making it easy.

"I wouldn't say no to Buffalo wings, but mild if possible. Ranch or blue cheese is good. And I hate mushrooms, beets, and uncooked tomatoes."

Lucky had the nerve to smile at me then, so I did the only thing I could think of: I went back into the house.

My duffle and the shopping bag caught my attention once I was inside. "Did you finish changing the sheets?" I asked.

"Yeah," she said, "but I was hoping to grab a few things out of there first. So I can stay out of your way."

I gestured for her to go ahead and turned back to the bags. I looked in the shopping bag and was startled to see it was full of books. Some were mine, but others were...

"Crossword puzzles?" I asked when she came back to the living room.

"I can't let you have your phone, so I thought those might help. I didn't know what level of difficulty you like, so I bought a few." Lucky blushed.

"And my books? I told your aunt I didn't need them after all. Can't work in that article if I'm just going to forget what I read. Did she forget to tell you?" I was confused.

"Oh, no. I didn't talk to Shannon. I saw them on your desk and thought you might like something to do besides stare at the walls, do crosswords, eat, and sleep." She squirmed visibly. "Didn't realize they were for an article. Thought they were pleasure reading since I didn't see a lot of other kinds of books around your place. I didn't want to dig too deeply."

I watched at least a dozen different emotions flash across Lucky's face. I couldn't identify all of them, but anxiety and anger were definitely in the mix. I hated how beautiful she was, even with her face twisting around as she fought what looked like a maelstrom of feelings.

"I've spent the last decade concentrating on work to the exclusion of almost everything else, remember?" I didn't know what else to say. I hoped that my mixed emotions weren't showing as readily as Lucky's had. I decided to treat Lucky like I would a student in a freshmen class, putting on my professor armor to hide the mess I was feeling. I didn't want her to know that, even amidst my justified anger, I still found her charming.

"There's plenty of garbage books on my shelves if you're interested." Lucky shrugged, looking embarrassed.

I found myself opening my stupid mouth and being kind. "When I was fresh out of undergrad, I worked at a bookstore for about a year. Had a regular customer who read nothing but Harlequin Romance and the like. I don't remember why she said this to me, but I do remember her telling me that 'a good book is the one you enjoy.' No such thing as a garbage book."

Lucky gave me a soft smile then, which, of course, pissed me off even more. I couldn't be around her.

"Are you done in the bedroom? I'd like to be alone now."

Her expression grew serious again and she nodded. "Bear should be back around noon, but if you're hungry or thirsty before that, anything in the kitchen is fair game."

I headed down the hallway, vowing to myself that I wasn't leaving the bedroom before she was gone unless I felt like I was going to pee in my pants.

With the door closed between me and the cause of my forced, offline vacation, I sagged into the chair next to her bed. The room still smelled of her. Of course it did. Maybe I'd find some air freshener or a candle to burn when she left for work. In the meantime, I opened the bags to see what Lucky had grabbed from my apartment.

There was more than enough clothing to last me the week. She'd even included some of my racier underwear, like the red lace bra I only wore on special occasions. I blushed at the thought of her going through my underthings, but then got angry at myself. It also looked like she'd grabbed all the toiletries I owned, including makeup, not just the stuff I used regularly. That fact finally got me to smile.

The reusable shopping bag disgorged three crossword collections, the books that had been on my coffee table—including the book of Jewish folklore—an enormous York Peppermint Patty, and a bed pillow–shaped stuffed animal that vaguely had the features of a dinosaur or a dragon. For a brief, very brief, moment, I felt a wave of sadness. I wanted to learn more about real, live leprechauns. Even more, I wanted to get to know Lucky better, to build on the incandescent spark between us, to go on an actual date with this seemingly incredible woman. The moment of sadness was quickly burned away by rage. Lucky had robbed both of us of what we might have become. How dare she try to make better something that would never be better? It would just be erased.

I shoved all her gifts, including the crossword collections, back into the reusable shopping bag and tossed the bag into Lucky's closet. Then, thinking about all the boredom I was facing without any work to do, I checked my wallet for cash and counted out enough to pay her back for one of the crossword collections. I set the money on the top of her dresser with a note. I might not have my keys or my phone, but I was determined to hang onto my dignity. Satisfied, I sat on the edge of the bed and started working on the first puzzle in the collection.

I didn't notice time passing once I got really in the puzzle. I was always like that, and I was glad. I needed the escape. I didn't come up for air until I heard a car outside. Less than five minutes later, there was a knock at the bedroom door.

I tucked my pencil into the book and put it aside. "Come in."

The door opened to reveal Bear. "I have wings, salads, fries, and beer for us." He grinned. "Lunch time."

I followed him down the hallway to the small, eat-in kitchen. He'd set us up with plates, napkins, and had even poured the beer into pint glasses.

"Classy."

"Lucky told me your spice preference, which is perfect. I also prefer my wings pretty mild. If you changed your mind and want more heat, I think Lucky probably has some hot sauce around somewhere." He sat and took the lids off the to go containers he'd placed between us.

"No. I like mild. I'm pretty wimpy all around when it comes to spice. My family's been in Rochester for generations. Like, a hundred and sixty years. But I always get mild wings. Thanks."

We dug in, and the wings were indeed some of the best I'd had. The spicy, buttery goodness of the sauce was perfectly complimented by what I thought had to be homemade ranch dressing.

When I looked up, Bear seemed as intent on his food as I felt, so I didn't try to make conversation. What would we talk about, anyway? The shitty hand I'd been dealt? My complete lack of agency in that moment? There wasn't any safe topic.

That was why I was startled when he cleared his throat after the first couple of wings.

"Something you need to know. My mother could have gotten someone to cover for Lucky today, but we both thought I should talk to you away from my cousin." The look on his face was incredibly stern.

"Are you about to threaten me?" I put down the wing I'd been about to eat and wiped my hands clean. I needed to be prepared to defend myself.

Bear ducked his head and opened his mouth without speaking, which made him look goofy. "No, I just want you to understand her a bit more. Hoping the two of you can coexist peacefully while we wait for Uncle Brian."

"Are you saying there's no hope of the satyr helping?"

Bear shook his head. "I managed to get Leander on the phone. It turns out that he's in Massachusetts for a couple of weeks. My uncle will be back before Leander and his girlfriend."

I nodded and picked the wing back up.

He started again. "The thing is, my mam's not wrong. Forgetting to reset illusions or letting your glamour slip—that's like an illusion for your person—is something lots of people do. I was fortunate and met my husband when I was a teenager after his family moved here from F... far away. And they're all leprechauns, so it didn't matter that I forgot the first time he and I spent the night together."

"I know what a glamour is. I've played table top role-playing games." I looked down at my plate.

"Lucky's not the only queer person in your family, huh?"

Bear chuckled. "No. I didn't know her growing up, but I knew about her, and learning that she'd come out helped me do the same. Fourteen years old, standing with my hands on my hips in front of the whole family. Told them I'm bisexual and if they didn't like it, I was going to run away and find my cousin Lucky."

"And how did that go?"

"My mam told me that if I was going to run away to live with a queer family member, I didn't have to go all the way to New Hampshire. I could just run down the street because Uncle Mike had a boyfriend and how had I forgotten that considering they used to babysit me when I was younger."

He laughed at himself and took a big bite of salad.

As he chewed, I decided to share my own story. "I fell in love with a guy in college, and we got married right after undergrad. I'm pretty much only built for monogamy, so I thought that was it. I wouldn't have to come out to my folks. But Phin and I divorced shortly before I finished my PhD classwork. Long story. When I finished the degree, I decided to move back here—aging parents, and honestly, I missed Rochester. The first person I dated seriously after that was a woman. I didn't actually come out to my parents until about ten years ago." I took a sip of my beer. "My mom was kind and open about it, but my dad..." I laughed. "My dad asked if that was why my best friend had slept over so much when I was in high school."

Bear laughed. "Was he right?"

"I mean, yeah, he was."

My phone sounded, somewhat muffled and distant, into the silence that had fallen after had a long laugh about my dad. "That's a text message." I started to get up, but Bear stood first.

"You stay here. I'm going to close the door, because I will hear it open. Then I'm going to go fetch your phone." All sign of amusement was gone from his face.

I did as he asked. I knew there was no way I'd get out through the barrier, even if I could open a window and climb out before he returned. A minute later, Bear was back. "Someone named Sam said it was nice to meet you and asked if you're busy this weekend."

"Sam? Really? We just met yesterday and he's already texting? I thought men were still all about mind games with this." I started to grab the phone but Bear pulled it away.

"I haven't dated in a really long time, so I wouldn't know." He sighed. "I'm guessing from your reaction that this is unexpected. I'm going to hand you your phone and let you respond— however you'd normally say it—that you are busy. Please do exactly as I ask, no more and no less. I don't want to be responsible for resurrecting old ways of dealing with outsiders. I like you."

He handed me the phone. I unlocked it and sent Sam a text that I was indeed busy and asked him to try me again in a week.

"Can't I just check my email quickly? One of my students might need me. Also, there's a really important email I'm expecting. Well, that I'm hoping for." I swallowed hard and tightened my grip on the phone. "A literary agent asked me to..."

"No," Bear interrupted before he took the phone back and, after he looked at my text, gave me a disgruntled look.

"What?"

He shrugged. "I thought you liked Lucky."

"Um, I did, but I'm going to forget meeting her in, like, a week. Besides, going home with the bartender isn't the same thing as a first date. It was supposed to be one night." I turned my attention back to the food in front of me. I'd been enjoying it, but this talk had spoiled my appetite. "What did you mean about old ways of dealing with outsiders?"

Bear looked uncomfortable then he sighed. "I don't suppose it will hurt to tell you, since it will be erased from your memory." He took a long drink from his beer. "Leprechauns aren't from Ireland, though a lot of us used to live there. We're from another realm, one that's commonly called a Fairy realm, that intersects with this one. There's a portal in Donnybrook, in the Dublin suburbs, that's guarded by some distant relatives, and that area was popular because it was easy to disappear to the islands off the coast. There's another portal north of Rochester, by the way, in Irondequoit."

I took all this in. "Okay, but what does this have to do with your implied threat?"

"Some of my ancestors weren't as careful as they should have been while visiting this realm, let themselves be seen without disguises, and that led to people trying to capture us for our gold. After a few humans were successful with their extortion, a rule was passed that no more humans were allowed to know we exist. We made the ones who'd already gotten away look foolish so people wouldn't take them seriously and started using memory magic, but, even then, there were sometimes people who we couldn't get to soon enough to erase their memories. Those, we killed. There's a reason the hills of Ireland are so lush and green. Besides climate, I mean."

"You'd kill me? Make me disappear?" My entire body went still and I watched him while I tried to figure out how to get away.

"We don't do that anymore, not really. Memory magic has evolved and can go out to a fortnight now if you're powerful enough, but before that, when we could only erase memories for a day or two, it was sometimes necessary." He sighed. "We're not a violent people. Just that we need our gold and humans kept stealing it. We need gold like you need sunshine or fresh air. Or vitamin C. We get really sick if there's not enough gold."

"I'm not going to steal her gold or your gold. I don't even wear it that often!" I pulled out my hamsa, my turquoise and *silver* hamsa that I'd been wearing every day since my grandmother gave it to me as a college graduation present. "But I suppose that's what a thief would say."

"Exactly." Bear sounded like I did when a student finally understood a difficult concept.

I almost laughed.

"And you think this will change how I act towards the woman who did this to me?" I thought about it for a couple of seconds. "She still messed up, Bear. She's still the reason I'm going to lose a week of my life."

"When he erases the memories, Brian will replace them with something else. Maybe you'll think you were sick in bed for a week with the flu or that you took time away from phones and work and slept out in the woods. You won't know you lost the week." He looked at the wings still on my plate. "Are you going to eat those?"

"Yes, I'm planning to eat the wings. And the salad. And I've barely had any of those fries that you've been steadily munching, and I want some. You think a figure like this happens by accident?" I gestured to my belly and thighs, intending it as a self-deprecating joke.

"I'm a happily married, *monogamous* man." He sat up straighter. "Besides, even if that weren't true, as attractive as you are, I'm not going to cross Lucky."

"What? I was making a joke about being fat."

"And I ignored it because I can see why Lucky was drawn to you." He patted my knee then sat back. "Go ahead and eat the rest of your lunch. We'll be here for the next ten hours or so. Want to watch a movie after? Lucky's got some great stuff from the '80s and '90s in her collection."

"That sounds great, but about Lucky..."

Bear looked at me. "Yeah?"

"I'm not going to be rude to her, but you can't expect me to be nice. I'm calmer now, perhaps because of the yummy lunch, but put yourself in my place. I have a right to be angry about this." I did. I really did.

He nodded. "So long as you're not going to go out of your way to be rude to her, that's all I can ask. She is my favorite cousin, and there's twelve of us if you don't count spouses, so that's saying something. I'm a bit protective."

"I can see that. Now, let me finish eating—which is a memory I wish I could keep, since these wings are just as good as I've heard. Then we can both go look at her DVD collection and figure out how we'll be melting our brains for the next however many hours."

Chapter Five

Bear ended up picking the movies since he knew Lucky's collection. We watched Matthew Broderick play hooky and Tom Cruise set up a prostitution ring but then I started to get twitchy so we moved outside and played cards. Our conversation never strayed back to Lucky, and that helped my mood. Instead, we talked about the movies we'd watched together, our favorite restaurants, and about how we both hated the Buffalo Bills not because of the team but because of how rabid the fans were.

Eventually, insects started to bother us, so even though there was still some light to see by, we headed back inside. We were just discussing which movie to watch next when we heard the unmistakable sound of a car driving up.

I met Bear's eyes and tried to remain calm.

"She must have closed the pub a little early."

I nodded. My little island of peace was gone and I didn't want it to get worse by fighting with Lucky. I told Bear, "Thank you for keeping me company while you played prison guard. I'm going to make myself scarce."

He nodded. "Sleep well."

I respected the fact that he didn't say anything about it being nice to meet me, since in less than a week's time I'd have all memory of this erased. I was grateful that I'd thought ahead and used the bathroom already. Hopefully, I wouldn't need it again until after Lucky was asleep.

I was going to have to talk to her in the morning. There'd be no avoiding that with as small as this house was. I knew I was being immature to want to put it off as long as possible, but that knowledge didn't stop me.

I knew, and truly believed, that me freaking out and getting angry at her again would only make things worse for me. I also knew if I saw too much of her, I would dissolve into a rage monster. That wouldn't be fun for anyone.

There were voices in the living room. I couldn't hear what they were saying, but that didn't stop me from trying. Eventually, I heard a car start and drive away. Bear was gone, and I was again alone with Lucky. I couldn't help sighing.

I settled in with the crossword puzzle book and was just starting to feel cozy when there was a knock at the door.

I sighed and tried to steel myself against any flashes of anger. After once again telling myself to treat Lucky like I would a plagiarizing student, I called out, "Come in."

The door opened. "I forgot to grab pajamas this morning."

"It's your bedroom. I can sleep on the couch," I reminded her. I sounded calmer than I felt.

"No. You're already set up in here." She pulled open the top drawer of the dresser and grabbed what looked like a T-shirt and shorts. Lucky turned to go, but then turned back. "What's this?" She held up the money and the note.

"That's what the note's for. To explain it." I pointedly turned my attention back to the crossword, but I couldn't make any sense of the clue. I was too aware of Lucky.

"No," she said suddenly. "Those are gifts. You can't pay me for gifts. I know there's no way I can really make up for what I've done to you, but at least I can make the time you have to spend here a little more bearable."

Putting the crossword aside, I finally looked up at her. She held the note and the money out in front of her like an offering. The look on her face was utterly and completely earnest. I wasn't a monster. I had to give in.

"Okay," I said softly, and Lucky gifted me a small smile.

"Okay," she repeated. "I'll get out of your way now, but tomorrow morning I'd like your input on a grocery list. I normally do my shopping on Wednesdays, but I can't really leave you alone here—what if there were an emergency? Aunt Shannon said she'd go for me, and I want to make sure she gets stuff you want and like."

"Okay," I said the word again and realized I should say something else. "But really, I'm not fussy."

She beamed at me but then seemed to remember herself. Lucky ducked her head, almost in shame, then headed out. Before she closed the door behind her, she muttered, "Good night."

I stared at the closed door and wondered how I was going to survive the next six days.

I woke to another soft knock the next morning. Unlike the previous day, I knew exactly where I was. Not in my home. Not in my bed. Not anywhere I'd planned or wanted to be.

"C'min," I croaked once I'd made sure I was decent.

The sun was fully up, so when Lucky stepped into the room, the light coming through the window turned her red hair to fire. Of course it did. Damnit.

She sucked in a breath when she finally looked at me. There was nothing about me first thing in the morning that was worth that reaction. Lucky shook her head slightly and cleared her throat. "Was wondering if you'd like some breakfast. I don't have any more eggs, but I have oatmeal and cereal and bread I could toast."

"Whatever you're having is fine." I pulled the blanket off and swung my legs over the side. "Do you have an alarm clock I could put in here? That way you won't have to do this every morning."

"Oh, I don't mind," she said, smiling. The strain around her eyes gave away her true emotion.

"I do." I'd gone to sleep wondering how I'd survive the next six days. At the moment, I was wondering how I'd survive the next six minutes.

As I watched, her face fell. I felt like I'd kicked a puppy. "Look," I said, getting up from the bed. "I know you didn't do this on purpose, and now that I've gotten some sleep, I'm a lot calmer. But, c'mon, this sucks. I'm trapped here with the person who did this to me. Of course I want to minimize how much time we spend together."

Lucky nodded then sighed softly. "I don't have an alarm clock separate from my phone, which I don't use that often since I mostly work nights."

I finished straightening the bed and thought about it. "Did my phone wake you up?"

"Yeah, but no big deal. I got the alarm to turn off once I figured out that weird puzzle thing."

I stood there and thought for another moment. "I'll talk you through turning it off until whenever your father is supposed to get back. And I guess it's not the end of the world if I sleep until I wake for a week. Not like I have a schedule to keep."

She stood still. I wasn't sure what thoughts were tormenting her, but the strain I'd noted earlier became more pronounced. Lucky's eyes flitted around the room, coming to rest on my chest for a second and then on my naked legs. Finally, she seemed to come to a decision with a small nod.

"I'll leave you to get dressed, then. Unless you want a shower, that is. If you do, I can wait for you for breakfast. Unless you'd rather I not wait for you and leave you to use the kitchen on your own." Lucky had her hands in the pockets of her jeans. She bounced on the balls of her feet as she spoke and avoided my eyes. She was clearly nervous, and I wished I didn't find it so adorable.

"I'm not planning to shower this morning. And you've given up your bedroom—I wouldn't feel right making you give up your kitchen as well."

Lucky flashed me a grin. "I'll see you in the kitchen in a little bit, then."

After that little bit, I looked over the grocery list that Lucky had drafted and swore internally. It was almost all stuff I normally bought for myself. Down to the brand and flavor of salad dressing and the fact that she included strawberries but specified only if they were local.

I added a hot chocolate mix to put in my coffee and a couple of cases of flavored seltzer to her list and handed the pad back to her. "I'm going to hang out outside for a while."

"Do you want some breakfast? Even just some tea?"

I thought about it, then nodded. I didn't want low blood sugar to kill my calmness.

A short while later, fortified by toast and Darjeeling, I grabbed the crossword collection and my sunglasses from the bedroom and went outside to the little seating area. I needed space from her.

I tried to focus on the next clue, but my mind drifted. I really did feel calmer—I hadn't been lying to Lucky. Besides, being a hateful jerk wasn't going to change what had happened; it would only make the situation worse. Seemed a good night of sleep and some time to relax, truly relax, for the first time in years was good for my temper.

I told myself it was for the best and then turned my attention to my crossword book.

I was still there when Shannon drove up sometime later. It struck me as unsurprising that this woman drove a VW Bug. An original model, too, in bright orange with a roof rack.

"Good morning, Mrs. Murphy. Nice car."

"Good morning, Professor Rose." Shannon gave me a piercing look, then her expression softened. "I bought it in 1972. Spent a ridiculous amount of money over the years repairing it and replacing rusted parts. Kind of a VW Bug of Theseus thing."

I loved that she made *that* joke.

"I trust you slept well?" The older woman crossed the yard to join me.

"Well as can be expected." I tucked my pencil in the crossword collection.

"And I trust you didn't make my niece cry?" Shannon seemed to be looking out at the yard but was also giving me ruthless side-eye.

"If she cried, it wasn't around me."

Shannon nodded her head once, decisively. She reached into her purse, pulled out an old looking book, and handed it to me. The cover proclaimed it to be *A History of the People* by Seamus O'Shaughnessy. "My Bearach said he told you a little bit of our history yesterday. Then, before I could yell at him, he reminded me that it wouldn't hurt for you to learn these things since Brian will be, well, you know. This will fill in a lot more." She slapped both hands on her thighs and stood back up. "Lucille mentioned you've studied folklore, so I thought this might be more interesting for you than any of the romance novels she has hanging around."

"Thank you," I murmured as I started to thumb through the book.

I felt Shannon's eyes still on me, so I looked up.

"We're very protective of her. She went on sabbatical to take care of her sick mam, and that was after her stepdad died suddenly not too long before her mam's diagnosis. Then her mam died and she came here to us, her tail between her legs, as it were."

I nodded.

"First time I've seen a genuine smile from her, one that wasn't at least a little forced I mean, was yesterday morning when she grinned at you. Don't squash that, okay?"

"Just because she's had a bad run it doesn't mean I have to be nice to her. If this book was a bribe, then I should hand it back right now. I'm not going to go out of my way to be horrible to her, but she's a grownup and so am I." I held the book out.

Then Shannon shocked me by grinning. "Just don't write in it or get anything on it, okay?" She didn't wait for an answer.

I flipped the book open again and turned to the title page. *A History of the People* by Seamus O'Shaughnessy was apparently published by King Finsk Press in 1952. I thought I knew every press that dealt in folklore, but then I reminded myself that this press might not even been in the human realm. I felt like dancing with excitement.

Sometime later, the door to Lucky's house opened and Shannon strode out. She looked over at me. "I'm not buying you an alarm clock. Even if Lucille pays."

"What? I didn't ask for one."

She looked down at the paper she was holding. "I guess that is my niece's handwriting."

"I told her I didn't want her to wake me in the mornings and asked if she had an alarm clock I could borrow. Then I told her that I could sleep until I woke and not to worry about it." I stood and, after thinking about it for a moment, decided to call Shannon on her nonsense. "And another thing, she really doesn't need her family running interference. Lucky—and I know you know that's her name, not 'Lucille'—is a grown woman who can take care of herself."

"Thank you." A soft voice came from behind me. "And, for the record, I didn't know they were trying to run interference."

I hadn't heard the door open. When I turned, there was Lucky. She was blushing fiercely but also smiling. I nodded at her, not trusting myself to speak without my voice cracking. I had the strong feeling that the longer I spent with this woman, the more I was going to like her. She owned her mistakes. She was obviously kind. She was gorgeous. And the fact that she was an absolute revelation in bed made her all the more enticing.

I turned back to Shannon. The older woman had a shit-eating grin on her face. "You're absolutely right. Except I'm not going to call her 'Lucky.' A 'chaun named 'Lucky' is too on the nose."

Once again, Shannon didn't wait for my response. She marched to her car and drove away.

"Why *are* you called 'Lucky'?" I picked up the book that Shannon had loaned me. I planned to take very good care of the tome.

"When my younger sister started to talk, she couldn't pronounce 'Lucy.' It was 'Looshy' for a while, but then one day she called me 'Lucky.' My mom thought it was hilarious, and so did my stepdad, considering what I am. I had no idea at that point. Didn't learn about

Brian O'Quinn until I was ten and I didn't learn about being half-leprechaun until I was fifteen. Thought Russell *was* my dad. Anyway, it just stuck."

I finally faced her. "You didn't know you were a leprechaun?"

"No. My dad and my mom split when I was two, and my mom remarried a couple years later. Russell and my mom decided not to tell me until they thought I could keep a secret. Not a lot of non-humans in Portsmouth, New Hampshire." She shrugged.

I was still confused. "Your mother married a human when she remarried? I didn't think that kind of thing was allowed."

Lucky's brow furrowed adorably, and she looked at me like I was speaking Russian or Kiswahili. "Why wouldn't she be allowed to marry another human?"

I sat. My brain took its sweet time wrapping around what Lucky had said. "Only your dad is a leprechaun?"

She nodded, still looking befuddled.

"I don't know why I assumed..." I stared down the driveway and saw a car drive by.

The silence grew. I became aware that I was holding the book in a death grip, still staring, and I wasn't completely sure I'd kept breathing through my moment of dissociation.

When I finally turned to face Lucky again, she had her hands tucked into her pockets. "I didn't mean to mislead you. I thought I told you I'm only half."

I thought about it for a minute. "I remember now. That first morning when we... Sorry I forgot." I managed to smile at her.

Lucky squirmed in place. "I'll go back inside and leave you to your book."

I sat again and opened *A History of the People* stared at the first page, but the words wouldn't penetrate my brain. I tried to read the same passage so many times I lost count and was about to give up when Shannon Murphy pulled into the driveway once more with her VW Bug.

She opened the back door. "Come make yourself useful, Janice. Probably half of this is for you."

"That was quick," I said as I got up to help.

"We're just five minutes from a grocery store."

The door to the house opened and Lucky called out, "Aunt Shannon, be nice to Niss. She doesn't have to do anything. She's a guest, remember?"

"Hmph," the older woman said at the same time I called back to Lucky, "I don't mind."

Lucky's expression turned bashful, and Shannon nodded at me in approval.

"Now get all of this out of my car so I can get back to the restaurant."

The three of us made quick work of toting the bags into the house, and then Shannon drove away. I appreciated her lack of blather.

Once Lucky and I were alone again, we stood there awkwardly looking down at all the bags of groceries.

"Do you, um, want help?" I asked. "That's a lot of food and stuff to put away."

Standing as close as I was, I could smell her shampoo. Another flash of lust hit me. I couldn't bring myself to step away. It startled me. When had I gone from blistering anger back to lust?

"No, Niss. You're a guest. I know it's not by choice, but I want to make you feel as comfortable as possible." There was steel in her voice again, replacing the tentative and overly earnest tone she'd been using since her family had shown up on Tuesday morning. It was nice. "But if you really want to wash dishes, I won't stop you." She bent down to lift a couple of the bags that Shannon had deposited in the middle of Lucky's living room. "Besides, I hate washing dishes."

I couldn't help it. I laughed, which earned me a smirk before she turned towards the kitchen. I grabbed a few more bags and followed her.

She looked startled when I put the bags down just behind her. "I don't know where things go, but I can at least bring them to the general area." I shrugged. "It's not in me to let you do all this work while I watch, so…"

Lucky studied me for a moment then handed me the bag she'd just been looking in. "Everything in there goes in the fridge."

It felt like a small victory, being allowed to help, and it left me wondering what other kinds of victories I might get to have.

Chapter Six

We worked together, quietly, until the paper bags were empty and in the recycling bin Lucky kept in her kitchen.

"Thank you," she said.

With a quick nod to acknowledge her, I practically ran back to the bedroom. That had felt way too comfortable, way too natural. Klaxons were going off in my head. I closed the door behind me, grabbed the book Shannon had brought, and proceeded to bury myself in it.

I wasn't sure how much later the knock on the door came, but I had gotten through most of the first chapter and had learned that Fairy was actually multiple realms that interconnected with each other and with the human realm. I'd also learned some of the—and this part fascinated me—possible scientific explanations for the portals that the author had encountered. The one I liked the best was that the realms were rubbing against each other all the time, and in some places the walls had worn thin. Like tectonic plates and volcanos and fault lines.

"Yes?"

The door opened just a crack. "Ham or turkey?"

"Huh?" Even as I said that, I realized I was hungry. "Whichever's easiest. I don't keep kosher or anything."

The door opened further, revealing the woman who was plaguing my thoughts even as I'd read. "Kosher? Why would you keep kosher?"

"You know I'm Jewish, right?" I looked around for something to put in the book so I wouldn't lose my place. "But, as I said, I don't keep kosher."

Lucky stared at me, her mouth slightly open. She looked like she wanted to say something but couldn't think of the words. Finally, she snapped her mouth shut and took in a loud breath through her nostrils. "I had no idea you were Jewish. Not that it matters to me. I was just asking which you like better. Because I'm making lunch."

"Oh." I noticed the note I'd written was still on the dresser. I grabbed it, marked my place, and turned back to Lucky. "I'm so used to people around here being overly sensitive and... You really didn't know? That's the whole reason they tried to set me up with Sam. Because we're both Jewish." When she looked confused, I added. "Spectacles?"

"I'm an atheist." She blurted out and looked just as surprised as I was.

We stared at each other until the moment cracked and I started laughing. Lucky's mouth dropped in shock, but then she started laughing, too. It was one of those whole body laughs and it left us both leaning against furniture. When one of us started to get serious, somehow the other would get them started again. Finally, once calm returned, both of us sat on the edge of the bed.

She cleared her throat and turned to face me. "Why were you laughing?"

"Just how ridiculous this is. Here we are, in the middle of one of the tensest situations I've ever experienced, and I've been through some shit in my life. My master's program. My PhD program. My divorce. But this tops the list. And yet, here we are, talking about religion in the most bizarre way imaginable. Because you were being polite and I misunderstood. Ridiculous. Had to laugh."

"That's what I thought." Lucky turned away. "Divorce?"

"It's been ten years."

"And this is more stressful?" She still wasn't looking at me, but I could tell she was very tuned in.

"Well, yeah. I am being held prisoner, after all."

Lucky nodded then sighed. "I usually put a slice of each on my sandwiches, also a slice of Swiss, with spicy mustard and some mayo. Oh, and I toast the bread first."

"That sounds perfect."

She stood and headed towards the door but then her attention caught on the book. "*A History of the People* by Seamus O'Shaughnessy?"

"Your aunt brought it over for me to read. Said I won't remember anything anyway, so it won't hurt for me to know. It's about leprechauns. Everything about leprechauns. History and biology and even their role in literature." I looked down at the tome. "I couldn't have cited this in my own book, but I could have tried to fold in some of his ideas about the symbolism of your people versus the reality."

"You published a book?" Her voice sounded strangled.

"Wrote a book. Trying to publish it. Well," I looked away. "Trying to find an agent to help me try to publish it. There's someone who seems interested, and I'm waiting to hear back from her, but who knows."

"I've heard that's hard." Lucky picked the book up and examined it. "Do you think Aunt Shannon will let me borrow it after you're done?"

"You know her better than I do. What do you think?"

She put the book back down. "I didn't even know this book existed. I think they sometimes forget that I wasn't raised around all this stuff. I only got quick yearly lessons from my dad starting a few weeks before my fifteenth birthday." Lucky raised her eyes to meet mine. There was a softness there that I hadn't seen before, and I liked it. "Do you want me to bring the sandwich back to you here?"

I shook my head. "I'll come out."

"I thought you wanted to spend as little time with me as possible. I don't mind if you eat in here, if that's what's bothering you."

I gave her a half smile. "I think I can handle meal times." Smart and kind and sexy. This woman had worn away my anger and was now working on my defenses.

"Give me ten minutes and I'll have everything ready." She stood still for a brief moment, seeming to vibrate in place, almost like a puppy that had finally learned to stay on command but who wasn't quite sure if they liked the idea. Then Lucky shot me an adorable grin before walking quickly out of the room.

I watched her go and didn't even try to keep myself from looking at the way her ass moved in her jeans.

After lunch, Lucky didn't fight me when I reached for the dishes. She even left me alone to wash them but returned when I was done.

"Look, I'm going to go a little crazy if I don't spend some time outside. I love this little house that my father lets me use, but it *is* small." She bounced on the balls of her feet for a few seconds, then gave me a direct look. "Do you want to go for a quick walk? We don't have to talk, it's just that I don't want to leave you alone."

"I can't go far. Your aunt's barrier, remember?" I wiped my hands with the dish towel and put it over the handle of the small stove to dry.

"No, I know that. I'd just hate for anything to happen to you if I weren't around to get you through that barrier." No bouncing now, and I wasn't sure what that meant.

I studied her, unsure what to think.

"Okay. Let me go put on some sneakers."

Lucky turned away but not quickly enough to hide how pleased she looked. I kept myself from sighing, but only barely. I wondered just how lonely she'd been that taking a walk with me made her smile like that.

Once outside, Lucky gestured towards the path we'd taken with Shannon when testing the barrier, and we started to walk. I was grateful Shannon had worked her magic—my brain hiccupped again over the fact that I'd witnessed real magic—so that the barrier was outside of this path. It was a perfect early summer day, sunny with a light breeze, and since our path was mostly tree-covered, it wasn't too warm either.

As we walked, it seemed like birds got louder when we approached, but not in the angry way that sparrows and finches did when I was alone. These were happy sounds. I didn't think the wild birds in the northern Rochester suburbs could be that different from the ones in the eastern suburbs, where I lived.

"Are..." I started to ask, catching Lucky's attention. She turned to me, and I forgot what I was going to say for a moment. I got lost in those green eyes. Once I'd gathered myself again, I spoke. "Are the birds singing like that because of you?"

She blushed and looked away. "Leprechauns are a kind of nature spirit. We're not cobblers or brewers or whatever folklore might say. I can't do much since I'm half human, but yeah—the birds are singing like that because of me. There's also a red fox vixen who's raising her kits nearby, and her den is under my father's gardening shed. And"—she paused to look around and then plucked a plant from next to the path that turned out to be a four-leaf clover—"these are true."

Lucky offered it to me, and when her fingers brushed the palm of my hand, I felt that electric and magical connection again. Lucky pulled her hand away quickly, murmured a quiet apology, and turned back to the path. I watched her go for a short moment before following. I felt again that sadness that I wouldn't truly get to know her, not in the long term, but now it was mixed with an oddly free feeling. I might not get to keep the memories, but there was nothing stopping me from making them.

I caught up to Lucky, which seemed to startle her.

"What?"

"Am I holding you back from what you normally do when you don't have to guard a prisoner?"

Her head moved back, away from me, as if I'd slapped her. "You're not a prisoner. Not really."

I stared at her and waited for her to answer my actual question. She stayed quiet, so I asked again, "What would you be doing if I weren't here?"

"I work a lot, but when I'm not working, I mostly hang out here. Go for walks. Read books. Watch movies. Sometimes I go to Aunt Shannon's place because she has a nice home gym she lets anyone in the family use."

I nodded and thought for a moment before speaking again. "Do you want to take turns with the leprechaun history book? I've finished a decent chunk already, but we could start trading off. That way, if your aunt wants it back when I'm gone, you would already have had a chance to read it."

She stood still in the middle of the path, quiet and blinking at me.

The silence built until I had to fill it. "If you don't want to take turns, then I'm pretty sure your aunt will let you borrow it."

Lucky grinned then. "I'd love to take turns. That's such a good idea."

I felt dazzled by her, and the impulse to press myself, especially my lips, against her was strong. I told myself, one step at a time.

We took another couple of circuits of the path, and when we got back to the house, I retrieved *A History of the People* for Lucky. She gave me another intoxicating grin as she took it from me. "Do you want to borrow a different book from me while I read this?" She gestured to a tall overstuffed bookshelf on the other side of the room as she sat on her couch. However, it was the book on the coffee table that caught my attention. The cover, in particular.

It was a traditional romance cover, just like the ones I'd read when I was a kid, with a couple in an overly dramatic clinch pose. But, instead of the typical Fabio-type holding a skinny and petite woman, it was two women in period dress holding each other. And one of them was decidedly neither skinny nor petite. The title was *My Windswept Love*, and it was an author I vaguely remembered seeing on the small popular fiction shelf at the college bookstore—Cat Stone.

I looked at Lucky, and she was blushing again. Her freckles did nothing to hide her emotions, to my great enjoyment. "It's just a bit of fluff. Escapism, you know?"

I picked it up so I could read the back. From the description, I gathered it was a fairly traditional romance novel script, a noble falling in love with someone from the wrong class in Regency England, but this was obviously a story about two women. The spine was so cracked that I couldn't read the title. "It looks as though you like to escape with this one a lot, unless you bought it used."

"No." She laughed. "I bought it new."

"Are you rereading it right now?"

"I finished rereading it a few days ago but haven't put it back on the shelf yet." Her blush deepened. "It's not serious. Not like the kind of books you have."

I shrugged. "I used to read romance as a kid. Might be fun."

Lucky jumped up from the couch, grabbed another book, and held it out to me. "I think you might like this one better."

The cover of this new book still had two women, but they were cartoonishly drawn and they were wearing contemporary clothes.

"Why? Is there something wrong with this one?" I held up *My Windswept Love.*

The blush Lucky was sporting deepened even further until I almost couldn't see her freckles. She was just pure red. "It's just that this one is a bit more literary."

She refused to meet my eyes, looking everywhere else she possibly could. I looked down at the book in my hand and let it fall open. The first sentence I read was someone explaining how much she "enjoyed the taste of a woman's quim." Something clicked and I looked at Lucky again. "Do you think I'll be offended if there's sex in here?"

Finally, those beautiful green eyes met mine. "I..."

"Lucky, I was face down between your thighs within hours of meeting you. You do remember that, right?"

She squirmed. I couldn't tell if it was because of nerves or because of the subject or maybe because of both. "I remember." The words came out as a croak.

"And another thing—the Freudian approach to analyzing fairy tales is rife with sex. 'Little Red Riding Hood' as a metaphor for psychosexual awakening. The thorns growing up around Sleeping Beauty's tower as a symbol of her physical maturity and pubic hair. I mostly don't agree with that kind of interpretation, but as a folklorist there's no getting away from sex." I didn't tell Lucky how I'd blushed endlessly the first time I taught undergraduates about the Freudian perspective. Just stood my ground.

"Oh." Lucky's cheeks had calmed to a fetching pink.

"Then it's settled. I'll read this one." I plopped down on the couch, kicked of my shoes, and tucked my feet up under me. It was one of those overstuffed cushiony kinds that looked like someone had microwaved a tufted banquette until it blew up like a marshmallow, and the fabric was a worn-down but still soft velvet. Cozy.

"You're going to read out here?" Lucky was still standing with the other book, looking down at me. Her color had returned to normal, but she still looked discomfited.

"Would you rather I gave you space?" I started to get up, but she put out a hand to stop me.

"Just that I thought you were going to avoid me as much as possible until my father returned."

I couldn't help the sigh that leaked out. I knew something had shifted in me. The anger and fear had receded, replaced with memories of how charmed I'd been by Lucky from the moment I saw her. I didn't want to avoid her anymore. "I mean, how big is this house? A thousand square feet? There's no avoiding anyone in a house this small. And this couch is way more comfortable than sitting on the bed or in that chair you have back there."

I'd looked away, but when I looked back at her I was gifted with a small but genuine smile. "Okay." Lucky bounced on the balls of her feet again, and her expression soured. "I really am sorry. About all of this."

"I know," was all I said.

"Do you want something to drink? I'm going to grab myself an iced tea."

"That would be lovely. One of the seltzers I put in the fridge?"

Lucky nodded. When she headed down the hall, I turned my attention back to the book in my hands. I expected florid speeches and overblown descriptions, like the romance novels I'd read as a kid. Instead, the story started with the servant spying as the noble woman allowed a man to kiss her in the gardens of a Cornish estate.

"Here," Lucky said. I looked up as she placed a mandarin seltzer on a coaster on the coffee table. She moved to the opposite end of the couch, looked at me briefly, then picked up *A History of the People*. I watched every movement, as fascinated by her as I'd been the night we met. I told myself I needed to stop being creepy, so I pulled my eyes back to the book. I read along as Molly, the maidservant, watched Lady Honoria and her beau, Lord Edwin, and wished she were the one kissing the lady. I was hooked.

When I looked up again, the light had changed. It was darker, though the sun was clearly still up. Molly had been promoted to lady's maid after the previous one left to marry the butler of another fine house, and she'd finally glimpsed the object of her devotion, Lady Honoria, in the altogether after she'd risen from a bath. Molly was furtively masturbating in her own bath, thinking about her lady's long and lean muscles and pert breasts. I was feeling the effects of reading about that act in such detail. I wondered how long I'd been reading, but when I turned to Lucky to ask the time, I found that she'd fallen asleep.

Like Molly, I took the opportunity to study the object of my desire. In repose, there was an unmistakable femininity to her face that wasn't as apparent when she was awake and in motion. Lucky's lips were parted ever so slightly, and I felt a bolt of want, a desire to kiss her that was overpowering to the point of pain.

I must have made a noise, because her eyes fluttered open. She looked around, and I thought about looking away but couldn't make myself. When Lucky's eyes finally lit on me, her expression warmed. "How long was I asleep?"

I chuckled. "No idea. I was absorbed in this book. Guess you didn't feel the same." I gestured to *A History of the People*, which was on the coffee table in front of her.

"Oh, no. It was fascinating. Just that I didn't sleep all that well last night." She stretched luxuriously, like a lazy house cat, and I managed to sneak a glance at the skin she exposed when she raised her arms.

"I'll sleep on the couch tonight. I really don't mind."

Lucky looked at me, confused. "What?"

"I'm assuming you didn't sleep well because you weren't in your own bed. This couch is plush and cozy. I'm sure I'd sleep fine out here."

"I..." She looked away, a slight blush creeping up from her neck. "I didn't sleep well for other reasons. Thinking about stuff. The pull-out bed in this couch is crap, but the couch itself is definitely cozy."

"Okay. If you say so. I meant what I said, though. It's your bed and if you want to sleep in it, you should. I can stay out here. Not like I can get away while you're sleeping, so you don't have to guard the door."

"Thanks, but I'm good." Lucky nodded, but still didn't look over at me again. She clasped her hands together, hard. I got the impression she was trying not to wring them, not to fidget.

"I remember." The flirt was out of my mouth before I really thought about it, but I didn't want to take it back. If anything, I hoped it would make her laugh. Break whatever was causing tension right now.

Green eyes finally turned to me again. "What?"

I shrugged and gave her a half grin.

Lucky stared at me and stared at me until finally she laughed loudly.

My grin grew. "You don't have to pussyfoot around me, Lucky."

She grinned. "That's the first time you said my name since we woke up to my mistake."

"Nuh-uh. I said your name when I was stupidly yelling at a woman who has and knows how to use magic because she insists on calling you something else."

The way Lucky looked at me shifted. The grin softened and, for a second, I saw desire in her eyes. Then, as quickly as I'd seen it, it went away to be replaced first by pain then by fear and finally by something studiedly neutral. I knew I hadn't imagined it, but I didn't comment. I realized I wanted her to want me, because I knew I still wanted her, but I didn't want to take a chance of pushing Lucky away. Just thinking about getting her naked again made me want to clench my thighs together, and I could feel my nipples getting hard. It was time for a subject change. If for no other reason than to get my mind on other things.

"Can you show me how the shower works? The controls looked complicated."

"Of course."

She led the way up the short hall, and I watched her go. After a second, I cursed at myself—the close quarters of the bathroom would make this aching arousal worse. Then I sighed. There was nothing to be done now, so I followed and tried not to stare at her ass.

CHAPTER SEVEN

An hour later, I was clean and in different clothes. And, most importantly, I was feeling calm once again. I walked down the hall towards the living room and heard Lucky in the kitchen. I stopped in the doorway and watched her for a moment before clearing my throat. Lucky startled, then paused for a moment to take me in. Her eyes zoomed back up to my face as a slight blush lit her cheeks.

It was good to know that I looked as good in my favorite jeans and low-cut tee as I thought.

Lucky cleared her throat. "I know it's warm out, but I was thinking of making baked ziti. I was going to just serve ziti with meat sauce, but I realized I have ricotta in the fridge from last week and I don't want it to go bad. I'm pretty sure the air conditioner will handle it. What do you think?"

I looked at her, dumbfounded, for a long moment.

I must have let the silence go on too long, because she said, "I mean, I don't have to make it. Just thought that since I have the time, I could do something fancier." The neutral expression was gone, thank God, but she looked nervous.

"I love baked ziti." I finally smiled at her. "It's been a while since anyone cooked for me, is all. Not even my parents cook for me. They get Chinese food delivered. Or sometimes Vietnamese. We're all addicted to pho."

Lucky nodded. "I like pho, too."

"Do you want some help?" I fought the urge to stuff my hands in my pockets and managed to get myself to stay still.

"I'd hate for you to get anything on that shirt," Lucky muttered.

"Do you have an apron I can borrow?" I was determined to push the point. There was no denying that I liked this woman. Now that I'd gotten over my anger, I wanted to enjoy my time with her. She was kind and funny and quick-witted. Besides, I'd always had a thing for redheads. And God, her freckles. The cautious part of me was screaming that it would all be a waste of time, and I could feel the weight of futility trying to settle on me, but also, I wanted to kiss every single one of these freckles.

"Fine." She sounded put out, but the grin on her face told me she wasn't. "I've already chopped up the onion and garlic and was about to start on the meat, but you could shred the cheese for me." She pointed towards the table.

The kitchen was pretty narrow, so there wasn't a lot of room to get by her. I managed to not touch, but just when I thought I'd gotten by, I heard her take in a loud breath.

"You used my soap?" Her eyes were big when I faced her.

"Yeah. That's the one thing of mine you forgot to grab. I didn't realize until I went to gather my stuff for my shower, otherwise I would have added it to the grocery list. I hope you don't mind."

We were still standing right next to each other, so I got to witness up close when her face softened. Lucky looked at my lips for a moment before speaking. "Don't mind."

Everything faded away except Lucky. Oh, how I wanted to kiss her. Or for her to kiss me. The heat was back in her eyes, ramped up to an inferno. I would have sworn she started to lean in, but then she pulled back and gave me a forced smile. "Let me get the grater and the cheese for you."

Tamping down my disappointment, I nodded and moved the rest of the way to the small dining table. I got to work, though I kept sneaking looks at her. She was unexpectedly comfortable in this kitchen, and as she cooked, the scents were making me hungry.

"That smells really good."

She nodded at me. "When my mother got sick, I had to find ways to get her to eat. To keep up her strength. Italian food always seemed to tempt her, even when she was fighting nausea from the chemo."

"How long was she sick?"

"About a year from diagnosis to when she died. It was metastasized by the time they found it and..." Lucky shook her head. "You don't want to hear about all that."

I finished the last of the block of cheese. "If you want to talk about it, I'll listen. But if you don't, no worries."

Lucky put a lid on the pan she'd been stirring and turned to me. She studied me before speaking. "Have you forgiven me?"

"I don't know." I shrugged. "But I'm not going to waste my time or energy being angry. It would only make this week harder."

The smile she gifted me with was slow in coming, but it lit up her entire face. "Yeah."

We stared at each other, grinning like a couple of teenagers. Lucky was obviously having some mixed emotions, but her grin felt like a good sign. "I'm done with the cheese. Anything else I can do to help?"

Lucky shook her head. "Besides, it's your turn with the leprechaun history book." She looked down at her pan. "Despite my falling asleep, I am enjoying it."

I made my way out of the kitchen, once again getting painfully close to Lucky in the process. I was assailed by the sharp, sweet memory of waking in her arms, and I barely stopped myself from sniffing deeply or, even worse, touching her as I passed.

Once I was outside the kitchen, I stopped. "You don't have to wear a human disguise if you don't want to. You know, if it takes too much energy or whatever."

"I feel more comfortable like this. I didn't have any non-human friends growing up, unless you count the dog my mom got me for my tenth birthday." She raised her eyes to mine again. "But thank you."

I nodded and made my way to the living room. I picked up *A History of the People* but couldn't bring myself to open it. As interesting as it was, especially to my folklorist brain, I needed to take a moment and think about Lucky. I'd been honest. I didn't know if I'd forgiven her. I did know that the attraction between us hadn't dissipated at the end of our ill-fated but mind-blowing night together, and I wondered if I could tempt her to bed with me again.

There was a series of beeps from the kitchen followed by Lucky walking down the hall in my direction. "It will be ready in about a half hour. Do you think I should make garlic bread, too?"

"Do you always eat this fancy?"

"Only when I have someone to cook for." She shrugged. "Do you think you'd eat garlic bread if I made it?"

"Is that a trick question?" I laughed. "Of course I'd eat it."

Lucky nodded, a soft curve to her perfect lips. "And where do you stand on the issue of eating in front of the television? Because we could watch a movie. If you'd like that, I mean."

I felt a momentary confusion. I thought she'd gotten over the awkwardly earnest approach. "You don't have to bend over backwards like that, to make me comfortable."

Lucky looked over at her DVD collection. "I know, but I was worried you might think it sounded too much like a date. You know, dinner and a movie."

"Didn't occur to me. Dinner and a movie at home sounds like a date night for a couple that's been together for a long time. Doesn't apply." I wanted to do a dance over her thinking that way. I leaned back on the couch and put my stocking feet up on the coffee table. "But really, what would you be doing right now if I weren't here? And don't say work. I mean if you weren't working."

"If I'd made myself this fancy dinner?" Her cautious expression was gone, and Lucky was looking at me speculatively.

"Sure," I encouraged.

She looked up at the ceiling and seemed to be thinking. "Probably drinking some wine and listening to music. Maybe reading whatever book I'm working on while I wait for the timer to go."

I jumped up from the couch. "That sounds amazing." I marched down the hall back to the kitchen with Lucky following me closely.

I looked through her small wine rack and saw she had a respectable collection of drinkable—though not expensive—wines. Even better, I saw a familiar label. "You saving this shiraz?"

Lucky stood in the door to the kitchen, looking at me with an expression tinged with befuddlement. "Not particularly. Our liquor distributor gave us a couple bottles to say thanks since we placed a big order. Lou—another cousin—gave me one to take home. I haven't tried it yet."

"Wine opener?"

She handed me a waiter's key and then nodded appreciatively as I used it properly.

"I waited tables for a couple of years while I was in grad school, before I managed to get a paying gig at the school." I grinned at her. "Wine glasses?"

"Cabinet behind you."

I made quick work of filling our glasses and found myself babbling. "I drink this myself. Lotta bang for the buck. It's like twenty dollars and drinks like a hundred-dollar bottle. Full bodied. Plummy and peppery." I wanted something from her, something I wasn't sure she'd give me again, and it made me nervous. She was smiling now, but I couldn't forget that fear from earlier.

I handed Lucky a glass and watched her take a sip. Her eyes got big and she grinned at me. God, she was lovely.

Lucky took another sip. "This is going to taste amazing with the ziti. You know folklore. You know wine. Anything you don't know, Dr. Rose?"

"No idea how to change the oil in my car." I took a small sip of the wine and let the richness of the flavor wash over me. "Now, I believe you said something about music?"

Lucky laughed, a low sound that was similar to how she'd laughed when we were in bed together. "Any requests?"

"Whatever's in your CD player is good."

She opened her mouth then closed it again. Lucky studied me for a beat then shrugged. "Why not?"

I followed her back out to the living room and watched her press *Play*. Aretha Franklin's "Do Right Woman, Do Right Man" filled the space.

"Really?" I looked at her.

"I was missing my mom the other day. She loved Motown."

I felt a strong urge to kiss her again. "I love Motown, too." I started to sway to the music. "Just that this isn't reading music. It's dancing music."

Lucky seemed to agree, because she started swaying to the rhythm as well. So, there we were, drinking delicious wine, dancing to great music. I was enjoying myself so much I thought I might start giggling with the glee of it. The only thing that would make it better would be if Lucky were in my arms.

A few songs later, the kitchen timer beeped and Lucky put her glass down. "Gotta take the foil off and put it back in the oven for a bit."

"That's another thing I can't do. Not much of a cook." I watched her go, once again enjoying the sway of her hips.

When the timer sounded a second time a short while later, Lucky disappeared again. This time when she came back, she had the bottle with her to top off our glasses. "It needs to cool for about ten minutes, so I'm going to go make the garlic bread. Nothing fancy, though, since I didn't order a baguette when Shannon did our grocery shopping. Just some sliced bread." She took a long drink from her glass. "Look over the DVDs and see if there's anything in particular you want to watch?"

Lucky had her DVDs arranged by genre. That was how I organized my collection, too, and it gave me a warm feeling to see our minds worked similarly. Then I had to fight off a wave of sadness that nothing could come of this connection we were building. It would be erased.

As I continued to peruse, I noticed she had one of the hottest sapphic movies of all time, *Bound*. I thought about it for a heartbeat, but then moved on. I might have been playing around with the idea of seducing her again, but that would be too obvious. Uncomfortable, even. Especially if she wasn't interested. I noted that Lucky had all of my lesbian and sapphic favorites. *Claire of the Moon* and *Desert*

Hearts and *Fried Green Tomatoes*. None of these would suit, so I kept browsing.

"Oh my *God*, Lucky! You have *The Blues Brothers*?" I called out to her.

"Yeah," she shouted back. "Love Dan Akroyd."

"We are *so* watching this!" I all but ran down the hallway. "I haven't seen this movie in years."

Lucky slid a tray into her toaster oven, then turned to grin at me. "Then we should definitely watch it."

I saw the baked ziti resting on the top of the stove. It looked golden and bubbly and delicious. This woman was amazing.

It turned out Lucky had dinner trays, so we ate our dinner in front of the television while watching Dan Akroyd in one of his best films ever. I was engrossed in the story, but not oblivious to my companion. There were a few times when I could have sworn Lucky was looking at me, but when I turned to face her, she was watching the television.

When the movie ended, we sat there in an awkward silence as first the credits rolled, and then the DVD menu came back up.

"I'm going to go wash those dishes," I announced. I halfway expected her to tell me not to, but when I moved to grab her plate, she didn't stop me.

I looked over and found she had fallen asleep against the other end of the couch.

I moved around as quietly as I could manage and got all the dishes into the kitchen without waking her. I had just gotten one half of the sink full with hot, soapy water when Lucky appeared at the kitchen door.

"I fell asleep during *The Blues Brothers*. How?"

She stretched her arms up and yawned hugely. There was a flash of taught skin as her shirt rode up. I told myself not to look, but I still did. I remembered licking across that part of her abdomen the night I came home with her.

I forcibly pulled my attention back to the sink and started scrubbing. "You must have needed it. Are you sure you don't want me to sleep out there? I don't mind."

"I'm sure. The couch is plenty comfy. I just stayed up too late is all."

She came into the kitchen and opened the fridge to grab a bottle of water, standing right next to me to do it. This close, I imagined that I could smell her shampoo, that I could smell her. I wanted to take a deep sniff, but I didn't.

She peered over my shoulder into the sink. "One of the few things I don't like about this house is that the kitchen is too small for a dishwasher. Not even a countertop one would fit."

I focused on the dishes. I had to, otherwise I might just kiss her.

"Shannon picked up some more mint chocolate chip for us. If you'd like some." Lucky was leaning against the fridge, casual as anything and still in kissing range.

"I'm actually pretty full still, but thanks." I turned back to the sink and realized that I'd already washed everything that didn't need to soak. I let the water out and cleaned up the inevitable mess I made while washing dishes.

"Do you, uh, maybe want to watch another movie?" Lucky was studying her water intently.

I wasn't tired, not really, but I also wasn't ready to make a move on Lucky. If I were to spend the next couple of hours on a couch with her, I didn't think I could avoid giving myself away. Maybe I was making too much of the apprehension I'd seen on her face, but I didn't want to push. Not yet.

So, I fibbed.

"I'm actually pretty beat myself, so I think I'm going to bed now." I smiled to soften my words, and I must have caught her off guard because she blinked at me, bemused. "You mind if I use the bathroom first? Brush my teeth and all that?" I returned the towel I'd been using to the oven handle.

"Nah. Go for it." She yawned again. The woman was adorable. "You mind if I keep hold of *A History of the People*? I didn't finish the chapter I'm working on yet."

"Nope. And feel free to read the next chapter if you don't fall asleep reading again." I found myself rooted to the spot. I didn't want to step away from her. I wanted to kiss her good night. Spending two whole days in her company, minus the time she'd been at work, was doing something to me. I had to think about how I was going to convince her to sleep with me again. There was no way I wasn't going to try to get her in bed again before I lost my chance forever. But the moment wasn't right. "Well, good night."

"Wait a second," Lucky murmured before reaching out towards my face.

I stilled completely, not even breathing, as Lucky brushed her thumb over my left cheek. She held her hand up for me to see. "You had an eyelash."

"Thanks," I managed to squeak out.

She finally moved away from the kitchen door so I could pass, but not until we'd stared at each other for another couple of beats.

I dragged myself through my bedtime routine, brushing my teeth, washing my face, changing into my pajamas, and putting my hair up in a ponytail for bed. I was feeling restless, so when I heard the bathroom door close, I peeked out and then went to grab *My Windswept Love*. If I wasn't going to be able to sleep, I figured I might as well keep myself entertained.

Chapter Eight

I wasn't sure what time it was, but it was definitely still dark outside when the door to the bedroom creaked open to reveal Lucky in a long linen nightgown. Never would have guessed Lucky as the nightgown type. I looked at her through eyes opened just a slit. Why was she in here?

A heartbeat later, I got my answer. The owner of the bed where I slept pulled back the blanket and climbed in with me. Lucky touched my shoulder gently. "Niss," she whispered. "Niss, wake up."

"'m awake. Whas wrong?"

"Couldn't bear to be away from you anymore. Need to touch you. Taste you." She captured my lips and kissed me fiercely.

When she pulled back for air, I stared up at her. I couldn't quite make out her features, but the feel of her in my arms was unmistakable. "What are we doing?"

"Isn't this what you want?" She kissed down my neck, setting my body on fire. "I'll stop if you want me to."

"God, no. Don't stop. I want you so much." I managed to twist around so I could remove my nightgown and my underwear. "So much."

Lucky followed suit and I moaned at the sight. It must have been close to dawn when she came in, because it was growing light. More quickly than I would have anticipated, but I wasn't concerned. It meant I was getting to see her freckled masterpiece of a body in the daylight. I moaned loudly as she kissed her way down my body. She nudged my knees apart and licked me from front to back.

There was a knocking sound somewhere, but I was doing my damnedest to ignore it.

"Are you okay in there?" It was Lucky's voice, but it couldn't be Lucky because her mouth was pressed against my pussy. "I know you said not to wake you, but it sounds like you're having a nightmare."

I opened my eyes to see Lucky at the door. The mist of the dream fell away, and I wanted to cry. It had felt so real, but with actual reality creeping back in I knew it for what it had been—a recreation of the incredibly hot sex scene between Honoria and Molly that I'd read before getting myself off and finally falling to sleep. In my mind, Honoria looked a lot like the woman staring at me, and Molly was definitely me.

"I'm okay," I told her. "Thanks for checking."

I didn't want to thank her. I wanted to curse her for interrupting a gorgeous, erotic dream about her. I also wanted her to go away so I wasn't quite so tempted to try to make the dream come true.

"It's almost ten. Do you think you're getting up? I can make another pot of coffee." She watched me from the doorway, and I wanted nothing so much as to leap out of bed, kiss her, and pull her back between the sheets with me.

"Yeah. That would be great. Thanks."

Then I was alone again. On the one hand, my memories of this week were definitely getting erased to be overwritten with a pleasant fiction that fit the circumstances, if Shannon's story about Carlos Santana was anything by which to judge. So, really, nothing I did mattered.

On the other hand, I craved her. If I didn't get Lucky into bed with me again, I was going to spontaneously combust. And I didn't want to be responsible for burning down Lucky's house.

I gave myself permission play it by ear. If the opportunity to seduce her presented itself, I'd try to get the sexy redhead naked again. If not, I'd deal.

My decision set, I pushed myself through an abbreviated version of my morning routine. Then, bed made and face washed and body clothed, I made my way down the hall.

The smell of brewing coffee greeted me as I turned into the kitchen. Lucky smiled when she noticed me. God, she was lovely.

"It's almost done. I only brewed a half pot, so it's all you. If I have any more coffee, I'll be bouncing off the ceiling, and I'm getting a little stir crazy as it is." Lucky blanched. "Not that I'm blaming you. It's my fault this is happening."

She darted a look at my face but looked away again quickly. Lucky seemed like she was going to do a Tigger impression, bouncing all around, even without more caffeine.

I put a hand on her arm to calm her down. It was hard to ignore how the contact made my skin tingle, but I didn't pull away. I was intent on getting this creature naked, so I might as well get a start on it. "You're fine. And I know what you mean. Do we know what the weather is supposed to be today? If it's not going to rain, I'd be up for hanging outside."

Lucky swallowed deeply while looking at my hand. She took a deep breath then nodded. "Definitely."

I released her and stepped back. "Can you remind me where the instant oatmeal is?"

She reached behind me for the top of the fridge and came back with the apple and cinnamon instant oatmeal I'd requested. She could have just told me instead of grabbing it that way, which was encouraging, but then she blushed and handed it to me while stepping away.

"Hurry up and eat your breakfast. You've fallen way behind in our book club," Lucky announced brightly.

"Oh?"

"I finished chapter three." She leaned against the doorframe. "And chapter four is about the move away from Ayrie, the land on the Fairy side that roughly corresponds to Ireland, to other parts of Fairy and the human realm. I held myself back, but I'm dying to read it."

I laughed. "I'll do my best."

When I'd finished my breakfast and washed up, I poured myself a second cup of coffee and went to find Lucky. She was where I'd expected: in the living room, sitting tucked against one end of her couch and staring down at her phone with intense concentration.

"Something wrong?"

My temporary roommate startled then blushed as she looked at me.

"How do you get your brain to work like this?"

She held up her phone and I saw the unmistakable shape of a crossword puzzle on the screen.

I laughed. "It gets easier the more you do it. What are you stuck on?"

"All of it!" She threw up the hand that wasn't holding the phone.

I laughed again, absolutely delighted. "What's the clue and how many letters?"

Lucky let out a frustrated sigh, then looked down at her phone. "Spread. And it's four letters."

"Oleo, spelled O-L-E-O, although sometimes puzzle makers take license with it and spell it O-L-I-O, even though that's really a different word." I felt like a conquering hero with the way Lucky beamed at me after she typed it into her phone.

"They spelled it with an E."

I spotted *A History of the People* on the coffee table and noted, not for the first time, that it had two bookmarks in it. It was the kind of thing I'd always imagined doing with the person I was dating but had never actually experienced. Something about it made my chest feel tight, but in a good way.

Grabbing the book, I pointed towards the door with my coffee. "Shall we?"

We spent the next couple of hours companionably, me reading *A History of the People* and Lucky getting steadily better with crossword clues. I taught her a handful of words that tended to show up frequently in puzzles and the clues most people used, like "sky bear" for "ursa," in between stealing glances at her.

I tried not to think about how I was probably the happiest I'd been in years, because I knew that train of thought was on a track with rails that led over a cliff. I'd spent three nights in this house and, at most, had four more before I was going to be kicked back to the loneliness of my own life. I was determined to enjoy the time I had here.

"You ready for lunch?" Lucky interrupted my thoughts. "I know it hasn't been long since you ate breakfast, but I'm starting to get hungry." I'd made it through the two chapters and had caught up to Lucky's bookmark—mine was a white slip of paper, while Lucky's was a proper bookmark with a fancifully drawn dragon on it—but couldn't seem to concentrate anymore.

"I could eat."

She leaned towards me over the armrest of her chair. "How do you feel about leftover baked ziti?" I had to remind myself to pay attention to the words she was saying because, leaned over the way she was, I could see down her shirt to the sports bra that was cupping her breasts the way I wanted to.

"I feel excellent about leftover baked ziti."

"Great." Lucky grinned as she leaped up out of the chair. "You wanna eat out here or in the house?"

"It's getting pretty hot out here, so maybe inside if that's okay with you."

She bowed deeply in front of my chair. "Whatever m'lady desires."

Hearing that from her was like hearing a record scratch in my head. Had she done that on purpose? That sounded straight out of *My Windswept Love*. When she stood up again, I noticed she was blushing. Definitely not intentional, then.

I decided to give her an out. "Reading about your people in human history giving you ideas?" I asked as I followed her into the house.

"Perhaps." She turned to grin at me, but I was so close I bumped into her when she stopped, nearly knocking her on her firm behind.

I managed to catch her before she went down, which meant I was holding Lucky in my arms. In my arms for the first time since we woke up in her bed together. We stared at each other as my breathing went funny. I was convinced that this was my chance, my opportunity to seduce her again. But just as I was about to lean in and kiss her, Lucky stood up straight and gave me an odd look.

"Sorry about that." Her words sounded strangled.

"Oh, no. My fault for following so close." I tried to reach out for her again, but she'd turned and had the door to her little cottage open.

Just like that, she got away.

I shook myself and let out the disappointed sigh I'd been holding back, then followed her into the house.

"Anything I can do to help?"

"Nah, I'm good," Lucky called back, a note of forced jollity in her voice.

I berated myself for putting her in that position, but I still followed her. I couldn't help it. My whole body was still alight from holding her. I had to be near Lucky.

I watched her pull things out of the cabinets and the fridge for a few minutes before she noticed me. The smile she gave was overbright.

"I was thinking, someone should probably grab your mail. Don't want anyone to know you're not there and try to break in."

I didn't know her well enough to figure out exactly what was going on, but something was wrong. My mind went back to that flash of fear the previous day. From the way she was acting, I didn't think it was a good time to push. In fact, it made me think that intimacy wasn't going to possible at all and that maybe I should give up.

"Makes sense." I softened my tone, hoping that would smooth things over. "Who are you going to get to come watch me? Or am I going to be left on my own?"

Lucky turned from me and set a frying pan on the stove. "I feel guilty enough about stealing this week from you because I got lonely. I can't imagine how guilty I'd feel if something happened to you because I left you alone with no way to get help."

"Okay." I took a deep breath and decided to push through my discomfort. "Lucky, is anything wrong?"

"Not at all. But, if there's anything you need from your apartment that I didn't grab the first time, let me know? Like your soap, which you already told me about. And let me know where to find it?" She gave me another overbright smile. "I've got lunch under control. You can go back to the living room."

"It's just…" I watched her drizzle some olive oil in the pan. Her movements were stilted compared to how she normally moved. I knew that for sure. Time to put my horniness aside and change the subject. "I've never seen someone reheat pasta this way. I've always just popped it in the microwave."

Lucky's expression shifted to something more natural. "And lose the opportunity to heighten the flavor? This is the only way to reheat pasta in my house."

I laughed. "Okay. I'm a horrible cook so I'll bow to your clearly superior knowledge, but how does using olive oil add flavor? Didn't you already use olive oil to cook it?"

She held up the bottle of olive oil. "This is infused with rosemary."

I nodded, hoping to encourage more cooking lessons, but she stayed quiet.

"I'm going to go read more of *A History of the People* and wait for lunch. Maybe we could talk about the first three chapters while we eat?" Please, I thought, please take this olive branch.

Her focus was still on the pan, but I saw her lips curved. "I'd like that."

When she came out of the kitchen a short while later, she found me cozied up with one of the blankets she had left on the couch from sleeping there the previous night. I liked it because it smelled a little like her, but judging from her reaction to being in my arms again, I decided not to tell her that. "Air conditioning is a little cold."

"Oh, do you want me to turn it down?" Lucky's brows knit together in concern. How was she enticing even like that?

"No. I'll be fine." I set the blanket aside. "Is lunch ready?"

She nodded and headed back the way she came.

"It turns out you're going to meet another member of my family since Shannon and Bear are both busy. But don't worry, Bear's husband is a good guy." Lucky took one of the seats at her incredibly small dining table. I noticed with some dismay that she'd placed my plate opposite of where she was sitting. No chance for accidental touch.

"Oh. Okay." The food smelled amazing, but my earlier misstep was weighing heavily on me, ruining my appetite. Still, I picked up my fork and stirred the food around. Wanted to keep up appearances and all. "So, what do you think about the theory of the fairy realm and the human realm rubbing up against each other like tectonic plates."

I looked across at Lucky and saw her mouth was full of food. She gave me a closed mouth smile before she continued to chew. When she eventually swallowed, she shrugged.

"Sorry. I've gotta eat quick. He's going to be here in about fifteen minutes. Want to be ready to head out when he arrives. Maybe we can talk about that theory later?"

"Should I eat quickly, too?" Though the thought of shoveling food into my mouth did not appeal in the slightest.

"No," Lucky told me through a mouthful before chewing and swallowing. "You take your time. I actually promised the rest of the ziti to Padraig as a bribe, so you'll have someone to eat with."

"What or who is a paw drig?"

Lucky laughed, and it was a natural sound. Hearing that from her helped me calm down.

"It's spelled P-A-D-R-A-I-G."

It was my turn to laugh. "I've only ever seen that name in writing. I thought it was pronounced *pah dray g*."

Lucky opened her mouth to speak, but there was a knock at the front door. She looked down at her plate, which was still half full. "Crap. He's early."

"I'll get it. You keep eating." Even if seducing her wasn't going to happen, I could still be kind.

"Thanks."

I had really thought the continued attraction was mutual. But judging from the way she acted after I kept her from falling, I realized there could be another interpretation to her actions. She was trying to make the best of a bad situation, and nothing more. She was being a good host.

I decided to resign myself to a few more days of unrequited lusting. Maybe I'd go to bed early that night and relieve my tension while biting a pillow and dreaming of the muscled and lean redhead sleeping at the other end of the house.

I fortified myself with a deep breath and opened the door to a surprise. "Pat?"

Pat was the librarian at Pittsford College who worked with me to find obscure resources for my research. He'd even convinced someone at Trinity College, Dublin to do scans of a book that only they owned so I could see the text without having to hop on a transatlantic flight. He'd only been there a couple of years, but Pat had gone so far above and beyond for me that I'd even sent him a personal thank you and made sure his boss knew.

His face quirked into a half smile. "When Bear said 'Niss,' I thought it might be you. I can't imagine there's many people who'd shorten Janice that way."

He opened the screen door, and I backed up to give him space.

"I always thought it was short for Patrick."

The tall librarian shrugged. "Most Americans can't pronounce Padraig correctly. I've gone by Pat for a while."

We stood in the space inside Lucky's front door, awkwardly staring at each other.

"So, you're..." I started.

"A leprechaun? Yeah. Not really something I could tell one of my faculty members."

I laughed. "Obviously, but that's not what I was going to say. You're queer."

Pat grinned. "From what Bear told me, so are you."

I looked down the hall and saw Lucky approaching. I lowered my voice to answer him so we wouldn't be overheard. "Yeah, but I'm not very good at it."

"Thanks so much for coming over. I'll be quick. Don't know if Bear passed this on, but I need to run to Niss' apartment for a few things and to take in the mail." Lucky burped quietly then blushed. "'Scuse me. Ate lunch too quickly."

I wanted to kiss her, she was so cute.

Pat looked at his watch. "You can take your time. I told my boss there was a minor family emergency and I might need to take a longer lunch than normal."

"Yours is in a pan on the stove on the lowest setting. Should still be good." She turned to me, and the urge to kiss her hit again as she smiled. "Did you think of anything you need me to pick up besides your body soap?"

"My phone charger. It's plugged into the outlet next to my bed. I know I'm not allowed to call anyone, but if there's an emergency, I really do need to be able to answer. I'm pretty sure I heard it lose power last night while we were watching the movie."

"Will do." Then she practically ran away.

"But, and I should have mentioned this before, I'm almost out of body soap. So don't worry about that," I said to a closing door.

I stared at where she had been for a long moment before turning back to the kitchen. The food on my plate didn't look any more appetizing now than it had before Lucky shot out the door like I'd lit her house on fire.

"What was that?" Pat asked as he pulled the pan off the burner.

"You know her better than I do, but my guess is that she's regretting ever meeting me."

"What?" He stared at me with his hand stuck in a cabinet. "Regretting? You're right. You're not very good at this being queer thing." He resumed preparing his lunch. "Lucille O'Quinn is very into you. I'm just confused why she ran."

"Pat. No. Sure, there was a mutual attraction, otherwise we wouldn't be in this mess. But no, it's not still there. I..." I looked down at my plate, unsure I could get the words out if I was meeting his eyes. "I almost kissed her earlier. I thought..." I sighed. "It doesn't matter what I thought, because I was wrong."

Pat laughed, startling me. I looked at him, hurt. When he caught my gaze, he sobered. "She called my husband in a panic. Said *she'd* almost kissed *you*."

"What?"

Pat took a bite and hummed appreciatively. After he swallowed, he smiled at me. "Lucky is such a good cook. They keep trying to get her to switch to working in the kitchen, but she says she makes more money out front. I need her to teach Bearach to cook like this, even if he only does it at home. So good."

"Padraig." I said his name pointedly.

"Okay, so here's the thing you need to know about Lucky. Her life took a quick turn to shit a few years back and never really let up. When she moved here, she was slow to let us in. Cautious. Closed off. I didn't know until a couple of months ago that... well, maybe I shouldn't tell you this because she's so private, but I think she likes you and it might help. You see, her stepdad and then her mam died within a short period of time. I didn't know her well before she came here, but from what I hear, it killed a spark in her."

What Pat said made sense in theory, but it didn't match the woman I was getting to know.

"They died a year apart," I said. "And she's always smiling."

"Around you, maybe."

I felt a surge of hope, and the hope brought my hunger with it. I looked down at my plate again and wondered if it was still warm. "Don't tell her I put this in the microwave, okay?"

He laughed. "She comes by that naturally. My husband's the same way." He looked down at his plate, still smiling. "Don't tell, but I do the same thing when Bear's not around."

Once it was warm again, I dug into my food, feeling happier than I had since this whole thing started. Things were definitely looking up.

Chapter Nine

A little over an hour later, Pat and I were sitting in the living room, laughing, when the front door opened.

I looked up at Lucky briefly, then turned back to my companion.

"Don't stop just because she's back. What did Melissa say?" I asked Pat.

"Nothing. I mean, what could she say? He was right."

"You two are getting along well." Lucky closed the door behind her and looked back and forth between the two of us. I searched her face, but it was once again a studied neutral.

"We work together. I know Niss pretty well, as coworkers in different departments go." Pat got up from the couch and winked at me. "I know you won't remember all this, but the next time I see you at work I'll try to be friendlier. It'd be nice to have someone on campus to go to lunch with besides other librarians."

"And I'd love to have someone to sit with in faculty meetings who I could comfortably snark with without worrying about not getting tenure." I stood, feeling suddenly awkward. "Would it be okay if I hugged you goodbye? Or is that too much?"

Pat laughed and pulled me in for a tight hug. He leaned down and whispered, "And remember, she likes you. I think she's just scared."

We pulled away from each other.

"I'm sure I'll see you in the library in a few weeks. You're teaching all the summer sessions, right?" he asked.

"Yup. You'll see me. I was already planning to email you about bringing my classes to the library, even before all this."

That got me an even bigger smile. Pat gave me a playful salute, then made himself scarce.

When he was gone, Lucky looked at me oddly.

She seemed to shake herself before speaking again. "I know he's a librarian, but I didn't think he worked at the same college as you. I thought he worked at some community college or other."

I shrugged. "All I know is Padraig started in our library a couple of years ago. He always seems to be able to track down the obscure source material I want for my research. Things that there's only two or three copies in the world, and he's still able to get me access. Used to think he was just that good at his job, but I'm wondering now if he's using magic?"

Lucky's shoulders seemed to go down. "Probably. I don't remember if he has a specific talent, but we all—even me—can bring luck to a situation."

There was an awkward pause, so I filled the silence.

"You didn't bring the little bit of body soap I have left, did you? I tried to tell you it wouldn't be worth it, but you were in a rush."

"No. I didn't. I stopped at a store on the way back, but they didn't have your brand. Thought about stopping at a second place, but I didn't want to keep Padraig waiting." She stared at me for a minute, her expression a little softer. "You don't mind using mine, do you?"

Did I mind smelling like the woman who was driving me mad with lust and longing? "No."

The look she gave me then made my insides feel like they were melting, pleasantly, like a marshmallow over flame. Sweet and soft. Pat had given me the knowledge I needed to bolster myself and to gather my nerves to try to get her into bed again. But I was going to bide my time a little longer.

"I put your mail on that little table next to your front door. It looked like you had other things there."

"Thanks. I appreciate it." I tried to sound reassuring, but her expression closed off.

Time to try again. "Want to watch a movie?"

"No, I, uh, I was thinking about going for a run. Feeling a little cooped up, which I know is my fault, but I wanted to expend some energy." She scuffed her feet along the floor and avoided my gaze. "I can run around the path through the woods, but I won't if you don't want to hang out outside."

"Just let me grab my crossword puzzle book."

Outside, it was glorious. I got to watch her move. It left me as breathless as if I'd been running, too.

After she ran around the woods for a while, we went back inside and she took a long shower. Part of me thought about joining her in there, especially the part between my legs. The thought of her naked, water cascading down her body, was a tempting one, but I decided to behave.

I told my brain to shut up and focus on the next crossword clue, but the white noise of the water and the comfort of the couch got to me.

I must have fallen asleep on the couch, because the light was different when I opened my eyes again.

"Hey," Lucky said softly from her overstuffed recliner. "Seems like I'm not the only one not sleeping."

I didn't want to tell her that I'd been up late reading about two women falling in love and having increasingly incendiary sex. I definitely didn't want to tell her about how I'd fantasized about the two of us doing everything the women in the book had done.

I cleared my throat then sniffed the air. "What am I smelling?"

"Just a roast chicken. We don't have to eat it if you don't want. But I needed to cook it or put it in the freezer if I didn't want to throw it away, so I..."

"I'd love roast chicken for dinner," I interrupted.

Her smile broadened. "And maybe we can talk about what we've read so far?"

Happiness flooded through me as I grinned back.

After we'd eaten the simple dinner and had our rollicking conversation about *A History of the People*, I felt good and loose. More good wine and even better company had me in a happy place. It was time to take the next step in wooing Lucky for the second time.

"Want to watch a movie?" I swirled what was left of my wine around my glass.

"You're not going to insist on washing the dishes right away?" She was still calm and open. A little flirty, even. Almost like the woman I first met. "Thanks again for cleaning the dish I baked the ziti in."

"I may be a horrible cook, but I'm really good at cleaning." I grinned cheekily.

"Sure, let's watch a movie. I'll put these dishes in the sink for later while you pick something." That was just what I was hoping she'd say.

In the living room, I made a beeline to the DVD shelf and pulled *Bound* out of its case. One of the sexiest and realest sex scenes between two women in a mainstream film was in this dark drama, and if I couldn't close the deal otherwise, I'd take whatever help I could get. Pat had told me Lucky liked me, and I was counting on it. But the movie could help me seal the deal.

When Lucky joined me again, I saw the exact moment she realized which movie I'd picked. The next few minutes were going to be important.

She looked at the screen and then looked at me. "Have you, um, seen this movie before?"

I nodded slowly, letting some of the heat I was feeling show in my expression.

"Oh," was all she said before joining me on the couch. I noted she didn't leave as much space between us as she had the night before.

"Would you rather watch something else?" I turned towards her and scooted a few inches closer.

Lucky looked at me without turning her head from the television. "Obviously I like this movie, otherwise I wouldn't own it. It's just, well, won't you feel uncomfortable watching this with me? All the sex."

I scooted a few inches closer. "Would it make you uncomfortable to watch it with me?"

Finally, she turned those green eyes of hers to mine, but she didn't say anything. She just shook her head.

I tried and failed to think of something clever to say. "Would it make you uncomfortable if I tried to kiss you?"

All of Lucky's breath left her in a big *woosh*. "No."

I started to lean towards her but found myself tackled back against the arm rest. She kissed me fiercely, deeply, and I brought my arms up to hold her close.

A few minutes later, Lucky lifted herself and looked down at me. "Why?"

I laughed and reached up to push the hair out of her face. "Why what? Why did I want to kiss you? You have seen you in a mirror, right?"

"But I fucked up your life." She nuzzled into my hand.

"You made a mistake that is a bit of a monkey wrench, true. But it's also forced me to really rest for the first time in a couple of years—and I only took that time off because I caught the flu." I lifted my head to nibble along her jawline. I didn't mention how the memories would be erased, anyway. I didn't want to spoil the moment. "Besides, you're also really fucking sexy."

I felt her laugh more than heard it.

"I have to ask you something."

"Hmm?" Lucky sounded so happy.

"Why did you pull away when I tried to kiss you this morning?" I held her close and kept my tone low and calm.

"I've been through this before. Well, with kissing instead of sex, but I've been through really liking someone and her liking me, too, but my father insisting on erasing her memories." She took a big breath. "I was so smitten with Nia. I was fifteen and thought I was in love, so I told her about who I really am, but my father found out. Then, after, I tried to tell her how I felt again but lost my nerve. Lost her."

"You mentioned her before, didn't you? That first morning."

Lucky nodded. "Last I heard, she was married to the woman who was our high school class valedictorian."

"No wonder you were skittish about me." I kissed her forehead.

She lay still for a moment before speaking again. "Still want to watch the movie?" she asked.

"What I really want is to drag you to bed and do all sorts of unspeakable things to your body. But we can watch the movie first if you'd prefer." I held her gaze.

"Yeah. Let's do that instead." She sat up and then pulled me off the couch.

"What about your DVD player?" I laughed as we ran down the hallway.

"It'll turn itself off in a bit. This can't wait." Lucky pushed me against the bedroom door. "I get to see you in the daylight. I can't believe I actually get to see you like this," she murmured against my lips. "I can't believe I get to touch you again. I didn't think I'd be so blessed twice."

I managed to grab the bottom hem of my t-shirt, and as soon as Lucky realized what I was doing, she gave me space to disrobe.

Her eyes widened as she took me in. "You're wearing that one." Her voice was appreciative and almost worshipful.

"You like red lace?" My voice came out strained because she was tracing her fingertip along the upper edge of my bra, teasing my skin with a ghost of a touch.

"I've been burning with the thought of you in this bra since I saw it in your drawer." She cupped her hand under my breast. "God, you have great boobs."

I couldn't help laughing.

Lucky grinned at me. "I know, I sound like a sixteen-year-old boy, but really..." She paused to cup my other breast as well before lowering her head to kiss the valley.

"I'm glad you're not a sixteen-year-old boy, Lucky, otherwise we wouldn't be doing this." I kicked off my shoes then pushed her back so I could pull off my jeans and socks.

Lucky's gaze traveled up and down my body. She actually let out a wolf whistle, which had me laughing again.

"Your turn." I pulled the bottom hem of her shirt out from her jeans and splayed my palm along her stomach.

Her eyes fell shut and she whimpered. "Your hands feel so good on my skin."

"Then maybe you should show me more of it." I didn't want to wait another second, so I started to work on her belt.

When she was standing in front of me in yet another sports bra and honest-to-God boxer briefs, I wished I knew how to whistle so I could express my appreciation.

"I didn't know anybody else would be seeing my underwear today, otherwise I'd've worn something nicer."

I pulled her into my arms and planted a soft kiss on her shoulder. "You look delectable."

Lucky sighed contentedly and moved me towards the bed. Our feet got tangled and we ended up half-falling onto the mattress, laughing. I couldn't remember the last time I'd laughed this much with a lover. She pulled me up to the head of the bed with her, smiling down at me the entire time.

When we'd settled against the pillows, I looped my arm around Lucky and tugged her close. I didn't know why, but I felt a little lost when I wasn't touching her. And having her in my arms made me feel found. I gripped the back of her neck gently and pulled her in for a kiss.

And what a kiss it was. This wasn't tentative like the first time our lips had met, nor was it like the burning and fierce kisses of our first night together. This was an exploration, and we took our time. Our mingling breath grew more rapid as hands roamed, plotting courses over the hills and valleys of each other's bodies. Every movement I made elicited a new moan or shiver from Lucky, and she seemed determined to do the same to me.

Eventually, she nudged her knee between mine, pushing my legs apart, and I gasped. But I wasn't content to be a passive part of this. I tucked my hand under the waistband of her boxers and grabbed a handful of her tight, perfect ass. Lucky whimpered.

"Your body is amazing, Lucky. Never be ashamed of it just because it's not overly curvy." I pushed her boxers down so I could get a better grip. "Fucking gorgeous."

She went up on her knees and helped me take her boxer briefs the rest of the way down. "I want to taste you, Niss. Can I?"

I lifted my hips so she could pull the scrap of lace that was my panties off of me.

"I just want to be with you, Lucky. Whatever you want to do, I'm game." I ran my hand up her front, gripped the straps of her sports bra, and tugged her down to me. I kissed her, moaning when her fingers teased up my inner thigh.

"Yeah," she agreed before pulling the sports bra off over her head. Then she paused and ran the back of her hand over my chest. "As delectable as that thing is on you, I want it off."

I arched my back to reach behind and work on the clasp.

Lucky shivered as she watched. "Fucking goddess."

The clasp was barely undone before Lucky had pulled the bra off and captured one of my nipples in her mouth. My other breast was in her hand and she pinched, softly at first but harder when I moaned. "You do like it a little rough, don't you?"

I nodded.

"Good." She reached down to the juncture of my legs and cupped me there, hard and a little painful.

"Didn't you notice how wet I got when you fucked me with that strap-on of yours?" I taunted her and threw my legs open wider.

She laughed and moved to kneel between them. "I was too busy fighting my orgasm in a quest to make you come a second time." She kissed then nipped at my belly, making me suck in a breath. I normally hated when anyone paid attention to that part of my body, but with Lucky it made me feel sexy.

The light wasn't as bright in the room as it had been in my dream, but everything else was the same. Especially her between my legs, looking up at me adoringly. Lucky's face was flushed with her desire. All of those freckles looking so very lickable. I was burning for this woman, and she was trying to fan the flames even higher.

"It wasn't a nightmare," I whispered.

She looked confused.

"When you woke me because you thought I was having a nightmare. It wasn't."

Lucky nipped my inner thigh when I went quiet again. "Tell me the rest, Niss."

"I was moaning because it was a dream about exactly this. You, giving me head, right here."

She kissed the spot where she'd bitten and gave me a wicked grin. "I didn't sleep well the other night because I was masturbating to thoughts of you."

"Oh," I whispered.

She lowered her head and flicked her tongue against my clit.

"Oh," I moaned.

Lucky pushed my legs further apart and then wrapped her arms around my thighs. Her grin was evil. And thrilling. I couldn't seem to catch my breath. All she did was stare at me, and I thought I might come just from her gaze.

"I think I want to play a game," she told me as she rested her cheek against my thigh.

"Yeah?"

"How many times can I make you orgasm before you beg me to stop."

Breathing was suddenly beyond me.

"I think you'll make it to three before you tap out. How about you?"

"Do I get a prize if I can handle more than three?"

"More pleasure isn't enough of a prize?"

I wanted to tell her that *she* was the prize, that I wanted her for more than this week. But that wasn't fair. Instead, I combed my fingers through her hair and grinned. "If I last to four or more, you sleep in here tonight."

"But," she started to protest.

I interrupted. "With me."

Her answering grin was beautiful.

"Don't think I ever wanted to lose a bet more," she said before moving to taste me again.

The first touch of her tongue was electric. She ran the flat of her tongue up through my folds and hummed, a happy sound that sent reverberations through my whole body. "I could do this for days, you taste so good." Lucky spoke without moving away, so I felt every brush of her lips.

"I thought you were trying to make me come so many times I begged for mercy, not taunt me until I begged to come."

"No mercy it is, then." She went to work.

The first orgasm burst over me quickly, almost before I realized it was happening. Her arms around my thighs meant I couldn't move, could only take what she gave. As the brightness of my release spilled through my veins, it left me gasping.

I felt Lucky's arms tighten around my thighs. She hummed happily.

An aftershock coursed through my body and Lucky grinned then licked her lips. "That's one."

She let go of my thighs and started kissing her way up my body. She nipped and licked and caressed, and my whole body felt like it was on fire. Everywhere she touched, it was like being caressed by an electric shock, erotic and overwhelming. When she finally captured my lips, it was not a moment too soon. I kissed her as if my life depended on it.

She nudged my legs open again and snaked her hand between us. I felt first one finger then a second inside me, exploring. When Lucky bumped her hand into me with her thigh, fucking me gently at first but then more insistently, I thought I could see stars. I wanted to tell her that I never came again so quickly after a big orgasm, but I didn't want her to think I was complaining. This felt too good and I didn't want her to stop.

I looped my leg around the thigh she was pressing into me then ground up against her.

"Yes, just like that," Lucky whispered against my mouth. I could taste myself there, and I loved it. "The way your skin flushes. The way your muscles move. God, Niss, the noises you make when you come... so erotic. So enchanting."

She lifted her leg for a second and I felt her hand shift inside me, then I felt her thumb brush over my clit. It was already so sensitive that I cried out.

"Was that a good 'aaaah' or a bad one?" She leaned down to take a nipple into her mouth and suck.

"Good," I whimpered. "Definitely good."

I felt my second orgasm building strength. Lucky let my nipple go so she could kiss me again. "Do you want my mouth again? Or like this?"

I tightened my arms around her, afraid she would stop. "Like this. Lucky, like this."

"Yes, Niss, use my hand."

Her touch got firmer and she watched me through hooded eyes. I felt something wet against my thigh and realized Lucky was so turned on that she had dripped on me. That thought pushed me over the edge and I gasped out her name as my entire body shuddered.

This second orgasm tore through me, somehow deeper than the first. It went on for so long I thought I might faint. When it finally started to ebb, Lucky shifted quickly and brought her tongue back down to my intensely sensitive clit.

The shock of her mouth pushed me to start coming again, and I screamed.

When I finally drifted back to Earth, I found my gorgeous redhead grinning at me. "You were loud."

It was darker in the room, and yet I could still see her grin, gleaming down at me. "You're proud of yourself," I accused.

I wasn't sure when I'd loosened my grip, obviously sometime while I was in the throes of that third orgasm. I took a moment to pull her close again. "You feel good in my arms."

Lucky nuzzled into my neck and planted a soft kiss there. "You sure you're not trying to distract me from your fourth orgasm?"

"Maybe. But what about you? I want you to come, too."

Her teeth grazed my skin, making me shiver. "I have my plans for that. Something that will feel good for both of us. Just relishing you for a moment before driving you absolutely crazy with my boudoir skills."

"Boudoir? Are you *trying* to talk like a character in a romance novel?" I giggled.

Lucky caressed up my body to my neck. "I've been meaning to ask you, is this some kind of symbol? It kind of looks like a hand." I felt her tug at my necklace.

"It's called a hamsa. It's something I wear to show my Judaism, even if I'm not actually observant. Can we talk about it later when I have more brain cells working?" I was impressed I'd been able to string words together coherently, because I definitely wasn't back in my body yet. My breathing was calming down, but I was still floating in the clouds.

As I watched, Lucky licked her fingers clean. "You taste so sweet after you come. Did you know that? Quite addicting."

I laughed a breathy laugh.

"You're not quitting on me, are you, Niss?" Lucky moved to lay beside me on the bed and, even though I was still a quivery mess from my last orgasm, I relished her touch.

I turned into her and kissed the underside of her chin as I caressed up her back. "Not yet. Not until I've gotten you off a few times." I felt my energy return and I felt back in my body. "You taste pretty amazing after you come, too."

Lucky arched into my touch, all but purring. "How are your hands so soft?"

I grabbed her thigh and brought it over my hip so I could start working to make her feel as good as she'd made me feel, but she stopped me. "I had a thought for your next orgasm."

"Sweet woman, not yet. I want you to come, too." I nipped along her jaw and licked the shell of her ear. She even had freckles on her ears. "Every part of you is delicious."

Lucky shivered, making me feel powerful.

"I have a toy I'd like to use," she whispered.

"You already made me come, and hard, with a toy. Or have you already forgotten fucking me on my hands and knees until I lost my balance?" I tugged and pushed her until she was straddling me. "Not that I'd mind playing that game again. Just that it's my turn to make you explode. What do you think of sitting on my face?" I ran my hands up her thighs and tried to pull her closer.

"It's a different toy. Let me show it to you and if you're not interested, I promise I'll go with your plan."

"You'd rob me of this view?" I looked up at her, still in awe of the fact that *this* woman wanted me. "Fine, but I doubt I'm going to be up for anything other than tasting you."

"It's something I bought a couple of years ago but never got the nerve to use with the occasional one-night stand I managed while my mother was sick." She rolled to the side and pulled open the bottom drawer of her nightstand. Lucky pulled out a purple, phallic toy that had an odd bulb at the bottom end of it.

"What is that?" I was fascinated.

"This part goes inside of me," she said, touching the bulb, "and I'd fuck you with it."

"Are you sure it wouldn't just slip out? As wet as you are?" I teased my fingers up her inner thigh, which was coated in her juices.

Lucky shivered. "I'd happily grip it tightly. It's also a..." Lucky didn't finish her sentence. She pushed a button which made the toy start to vibrate.

"Oh," I breathed out.

"Does that mean you'll let me?"

I pushed her onto her back, took the toy from her, and gently put the bulb inside her. I kept her down with a restraining hand on her chest, not that she was fighting me.

"And what if I..." I threw my leg over her and lined the odd toy up with my own opening.

"God, yes." Lucky's hands came to rest on my hips and I lowered myself gently onto the device that now connected us. The vibrations weren't very strong, but the friction was still delicious.

She laughed, startling me. "I'm so scared it's going to fall out in a crucial moment."

"Then you better keep your thighs together. I was promised a fourth orgasm." I lifted up and lowered gently. My poor cunt was overstimulated and it hurt, but I realized I would be coming soon.

Lucky whimpered as I leaned back. I propped myself up by bracing my arms next to her thighs as I ground against the purple toy. Every time I bottomed out, Lucky let out the most decadent sounding moans and sighs. I stopped worrying about my own pleasure, and started chasing hers.

"I need to kiss you. I'm so close, but I want to be kissing you when I..." Lucky didn't finish her sentence because I captured her lips.

I circled my hips, looking for an angle that made her quiver and moan and, once I found it, I didn't deviate. It was brutal and erotic and all I wanted was to feel Lucky come apart under me.

She didn't make me wait long. Lucky screamed into my mouth then, her whole body stiff and her arms brutally tight around me. She collapsed after a long moment and looked up at me with dazed eyes and a slack mouth.

I was so close after that that I reached between us and frigged my clit once, twice, a third time, and then I was coming, too. It wasn't as earth-shattering as my earlier peaks, but it was enough. I almost collapsed on top of Lucky but was still conscious of my weight. She might love my curves, and I had to admit I didn't hate them, but I didn't want to squash this delectable woman.

"Can't... Niss, can you take it out? I"—she paused to quiver—"I can't take anymore."

Laughing, I reached for the toy, removed it from her still twitching body, and then turned it off. I turned her so Lucky was facing away from me and then pulled her into my arms. "Or do you wanna be the big spoon?"

"No." She pulled my arms more tightly around her. "I like this."

We lay like that for long moments and it was bliss.

"Do I sleep in here tonight?" Lucky murmured.

"What do you mean? Of course you do. I had four orgasms." I kissed the back of her neck, enjoying the silky feel of her hair as it tickled my nose.

"Technically you finished yourself off that last time."

"Are you saying you want to sleep on the couch? Because I should warn you, if you do, I'm sleeping out there, too."

Lucky twisted in my arms and looked at me intently. "I cannot stop kicking myself for how I messed up. I want to take you to the movies or to the zoo or even to a museum. You know. On a date. I really like you, Niss, and I wish I could date you. But your memory of all this is going to be erased, and if I see you after my father's back, I'll just be some random bozo making moon eyes at you." Even though her words were joking, I noticed her eyes were bright with unshed tears.

"I know." I kissed her forehead. "And, for the record, I really like you, too."

She nuzzled into me as if she were trying to burrow into my chest.

I kissed her forehead. "I'm glad Pat told me that you do like me, and I'm glad I pushed."

"Me, too," she whispered.

"And, hey, we can enjoy the time until your father returns, can't we?" I ran my fingers through her hair, trying as best I could to soothe her.

"Yeah, that's what I decided." Lucky sighed contentedly. "That feels nice."

"I haven't touched that enormous peppermint patty you got for me yet. Wanna share it while we watch cartoons?"

"Oh my God, yes. That sounds amazing." The grin she flashed at me made my heart hiccup.

I couldn't help giving her my own answering grin.

Chapter Ten

We spent the rest of the evening in our pajamas, on the couch, eating overly sweet candy and watching Lucky's DVD collection of Looney Tunes. Over the course of the first DVD, Lucky oozed closer and closer to me without ever seeming to move. A half hour after we started, she was leaning into me and using me as a pillow. I put my arm around her shoulder, eliciting a contented sigh.

"You could have asked me to cuddle from the beginning, you know," I said against the top of her head. "Truth is, I like cuddling, too."

Lucky giggled, a sound that I never would have expected from her, but then she tipped her head back and looked up at me. Her lips curled up at the edges, but the real smile was in her eyes. I felt trapped in her gaze and never wanted to be released.

Her delicious mouth was inches from mine, and all I wanted to do was kiss her. Then I reminded myself I was allowed to now, and closed the distance.

The kiss started soft and sweet, almost innocent. Lucky's lips brushed against mine and she let out another contented sigh. Then her eyes opened and she stared at me. I saw the shift of emotions from contentment to the beginnings of arousal, and I leaned in for another kiss. I licked across her bottom lip then along the seam of her mouth. Lucky's lips parted and I took immediate advantage. I didn't think I'd ever get enough of kissing her, and I only had a few days left before I'd lose my chance, maybe forever.

She moaned low when I pulled back to catch my breath. She whispered, "Every time you kiss me is like the first time. Like you're trying to learn me. How do you do that?"

"Trying to get in as much kissing as I can between now and when your father gets back from his trip."

"Just kissing?" Lucky traced the outline of my now hard nipple through the camisole I put on for cover.

"I could be persuaded to stop watching Bugs take the wrong turn at Albuquerque, I suppose. If you want to talk about O'Shaughnessy's theory of magic influencing genetics in the white ermine moth, I'd be open to that." I ran my hand over her shoulder and down the front of her t-shirt.

"Niss!" She laughed and arced into my hand.

"Or, and it's okay if you're not open to this idea, we could recreate Molly and Honoria's first time spending the night together." I pulled my hand away from Lucky just long enough to reach under the bottom hem of her shirt and palm one of her breasts. I loved the way her skin felt under my hand.

"You're not sore from how much I fucked you earlier?" She gasped when I pinched her nipple lightly.

"A little, but I wasn't planning to be on the receiving end." I licked into her mouth and tasted her next gasp.

"You'd top me?" Her eyes got big.

"If you'd let me."

Lucky struggled out of my arms and jumped to her feet then pulled me up after. "Let you? *Let you*? Beg you to, maybe."

She turned off the DVD player and the television, then dragged me down the hall to her bedroom. I couldn't help laughing. Lucky was just so much fun, and if I only had a few days left with her, I was going to make the most of every moment.

The next afternoon, we were hanging out after a lunch of Lucky's homemade pizza, and it was everything I'd always wanted from a romantic relationship. I'd never gotten it. Not even when I was supposedly happily married. This was bliss.

I put my bookmark into *A History of the People* and looked over at Lucky. My feet rested in her lap as she worked on another crossword puzzle. I'd given her back the easy collection because I found them boring, but it was nice to see her enjoying it.

"I didn't realize there was a long history of humans intermarrying with leprechauns."

It took Lucky a long moment to pull her eyes away from the puzzle, but when she looked over to me, she was smiling. "Yeah. Is that what the next chapter is about?"

"Well, first the author talks about how he thinks leprechauns' origins were partially tied to humans making it through the barrier and getting stuck on the other side, in Fairy, and the magic altering their DNA. But the section I just started is going to cover the fact that, well, intermarriage happens and has for a long time."

Lucky put her puzzle book down and scooted over to my end of the couch. I'd finally convinced her to leave off the glamour spell, and there was something thrilling about seeing her as she really was. There was a wildness to her face and body that made it hard to keep my hands to myself. But this topic was too serious for me to get distracted.

"Why can't we just date? I like you. You like me. Why *can't* we?" I could admit, at least to myself, that Lucky was perfect for me. I didn't want to lose her. "Why can't I keep my memories?"

"There are rules that say we can't." She pulled the book out of my hands and crawled into my lap. "I wish we could. Really, I do."

"Why not? Specifically." I put my hands on her hips, holding her in place.

"This is what my mother told me." She put her hands on top of mine. "First, the couple needs to be together for long enough that the clan trusts the human. We can date humans; they just can't know that we're *not* human."

I nodded. That made sense.

"Second, there needs to be testimony of the quality of the human's character. Spending time among the leprechaun's family and friends is the only way to get that."

"Your mom spent time with your father's family?"

She nodded. "They spent a lot of time visiting Rochester, but also my father has cousins in Boston, which is only a couple of hours from where I grew up." Lucky leaned forward and nuzzled into my neck as I put my arms around her. "I wasn't around them much, but they sent birthday presents most years until I was in college."

"What are the other rules?" For the first time since we'd met, all I wanted to do was hold her. No sex. No kisses. Just my arms around her.

"There was a kind of ceremony my mom said she had to go through, but she wouldn't tell me about it when I first asked because she said I was too young. And when I was old enough, she couldn't remember all the details. Just that she was surrounded by my father's family and there was a lot of noise." I felt her breath against my neck and couldn't help the shiver.

"I know for sure that my mom said she didn't think she'd pass their tests, and my parents had been together for a couple of years before my father revealed himself to her." She sat back and looked at me.

I sighed. Lucky leaned back, then cupped my cheek. A wave of sadness took over her features, making me feel even worse. It helped to know we were in this together.

"I especially don't want to forget the way you shook when you came last night." I was hurting, but I couldn't waste this time.

"That *was* fun," she agreed.

"To be clear, I don't want to forget any of this. I'm more relaxed than I've been in years, and I'm having an amazing time just being with you." I was normally more articulate than this, but from the curving of her full lips, it seemed that my point was made.

A sound pierced the silence, and it took me a moment to realize it was my phone ringing.

Lucky froze for a second, then leaped up off my lap and dove for the entertainment center. She pulled open something I didn't even know was a door, grabbed my phone, and answered before I could blink.

I heard my mother's voice—"Baby, are you there?"—as Lucky held the phone out to me.

"I trust you," Lucky told me in a whisper as I took the phone from her.

"Hey, Mom. I'm here." The phone was at my ear, but my eyes were still glued to Lucky.

"Did I interrupt something?" My mother sounded concerned.

"No. Just had my hands full so I couldn't answer right away." I congratulated myself on coming up with a reason that approximated the truth.

"Were you working? Aren't you supposed to be off this week, Niss? You work too much, baby. I worry about you."

My dad chimed in from the background. "Tell her the FROG is always available if she wants it!"

"You heard him, right?"

I laughed. "Yes, I heard him."

My mother sighed. "I wish he'd never learned that acronym. What's so hard about saying 'finished room over the garage'?"

Lucky watched me, but then she seemed to make her mind up about something and mouthed the words, "I'll be right back." She disappeared down the hall to her bedroom.

"I'm not working and I don't need the mother-in-law apartment." I laughed as I watched for Lucky to return. "Why are you calling? Aren't transatlantic calls crazy expensive?"

"Nope. The cruise company has that VoIP thing. Part of the cost of the cruise," my mother explained, actually pronouncing the acronym for "Voice over Internet Protocol" like "voyp." This from a woman who had just complained about "FROG."

"So why are you calling?" I asked again.

"Your dad and I decided to visit with Charlie and Annette after the cruise instead of coming straight home. We're having so much fun with them, and they do live right on the ocean. I know it's tourist season in Bethany Beach, but they have a big place."

"That sounds nice. But you know I'm adult and live on my own, right? I'm forty-five. I'm not your keeper either."

"Way to make me feel every year of my sixty-eight, baby. No, that's not why I'm calling. It's just that we had the mail held through next Monday, but we'll be gone for another four or five days and I was hoping you could pick the mail up until we're home." I wondered if there was a way to make sure this memory came through, then thought of something.

"Can you email me the specifics, Mom? I don't want to forget."

"You need me to send you an email? I can't just tell you?" She laughed. "I'm the senior citizen here, not you."

"Mom, I'm in the middle of something and I don't want it to slip my mind."

She laughed again. "Sure thing, baby. Oh, wait, your father wants to say hello."

"Hey, Nissy. I miss having you at the house. Someone to stick up for me to your mother."

I tried and failed to quash the laugh that bubbled up at my father's words.

"Hey!" My mom called from the background. "You be nice, David."

They laughed. This was their thing. They were still deeply in love, even after being married for almost fifty years, and part of that was teasing.

"We're going to Vienna tomorrow and I want to bring you some chocolate. Annette has been here before and has promised to show us this amazing chocolatier. But we couldn't remember if you like dark or milk or what."

"Anything with mint."

He held the phone away from his ear and yelled to my mother. "She said anything with mint. I told you, Becks."

Lucky came back down the hall then and I couldn't help smiling, both at her and at my parents.

"And listen, Nissy, we met a couple here who has a daughter—a nice, single, *Jewish* daughter—who's moving to our area. She got a job at the University of Rochester. Can I give them your phone number to give to her? You could help her get settled."

My parents had been awkward about my bisexuality at first, but then, somewhere along the line, they'd realized that meant there was a whole new demographic they could try to set me up with.

"No, Dad. I'm not going to let you set me up with the daughter of a random couple you and Mom met on your cruise."

Lucky moved to sit with me, and she curled into my side. I, of course, put my arm around her shoulders.

My dad sighed through the phone. "But I hate the thought of you alone so much."

I couldn't tell him I wasn't alone. I wanted to. Lucky might not have been Jewish, but other than that she was exactly the kind of person they told me they wanted for me. Kind and intelligent and devoted to her family. That's the kind of person I'd always wanted, too, but never found. Hell, that was the reason I hadn't run the other direction when Kim introduced me to Sam. Sex I could get anywhere, even by myself. But this kind of connection was too good to let go of.

"Look, Dad, I need to go."

Lucky squirmed until her arm was around my back and let out a soft sigh.

"Yeah, us, too. Dinner is soon. But listen, Nissy, let's go out for Korean when we get back. I'll buy you some of that soup you like and show you pictures of the Kendells' daughter."

I laughed.

"Love you, Nissy."

My mom called out from the background. "We love you, Janice Shifra Rose!"

"I love you guys, too, but tell Mom not to use my middle name unless I'm in trouble."

My father's chuckle was the only response I got.

"Have fun. See you when you get back," I added.

We hung up, and I handed the phone to Lucky.

"You can keep it," she told me.

I put it on the table beside me and then put my other arm around her.

"Are you sure? You made such a big deal about cutting me off. I'd hate for you to, I don't know, get in trouble."

"I'll hide it away again before my father gets back."

I tightened my hold around her briefly. "That was my parents."

"I gathered from the fact that you said 'Mom' and 'Dad'." Somehow, Lucky managed to scoot just a little bit closer. "You're so cozy." Her voice was low and I could barely hear it, but still it warmed me.

I looked down at my phone again and noticed the light was flashing. "Do you mind if I check why that light is going? I promise you can watch the whole time."

Lucky lifted herself away from me and I instantly missed the contact, but I still grabbed the phone instead of her.

I looked at the alerts and saw it was an email to my work account. I flipped to it immediately, worried it might be from a student protesting a grade, only to find an email from Courtney Smith at the Smith & Johnson Agency. My whole body froze.

"What is it?" Lucky looked at my phone. "Who's Courtney Smith?"

The voice that came out didn't sound like me at all. It was squeaky and high pitched. "A literary agent."

"Is that good or bad?" Lucky moved to rest her weight against me again. "You said you're looking for one, right?"

"This email could be either." There, that sounded more like me.

"Then don't you want to open it?" Her mouth was so close that I felt the puff of her breath against my ear.

"It won't matter either way. It's not like I can react to it until next week." I said that, but I didn't put the phone down.

I felt Lucky's arm going around my back again. "What's *Loki and Coyote*?"

"The book I told you about, the one I wrote based on my dissertation."

I felt her lips on my neck. "Have I told you how attractive your smarts are?"

"Do you want me to open the email? Or to drag you to the bedroom?" I wasn't complaining. I leaned into her.

"Both. In that order."

I thumbed the email open and scanned the first paragraph. "If you are still looking for representation, I would be very interested in setting up a meeting with you." I couldn't breathe for the happiness.

"I wonder..." Lucky muttered, but then stopped.

I marked the email as unread, put my phone down, and turned to face her. "You wonder what?"

"I felt so bad about everything that when you told me about your book, I gave you some luck. It doesn't make anything happen that couldn't normally happen, just increases the chances of a good outcome." She blushed. "Superstitious surgeons thought I was good luck in the OR, and they were right."

"You did that for me?"

"Felt I owed it to you."

I was about to kiss her when she yawned hugely. I laughed.

"You know I'm not bored, right?" She looked horrified.

I kissed her forehead. "How about I give you a rain check on dragging you to bed?"

Lucky nodded and snuggled into me.

After a moment, she spoke again. "Hey, what did your parents want, anyway? They need you for something?"

"Nah. I fibbed a little about them at the beginning of this whole thing. They're on a cruise right now, somewhere on the Danube near Vienna. They went with friends, people they've known since college, and instead of coming home they are going to visit their friends' place first. They want me to take in the mail."

"Hmm?" Lucky sounded half asleep.

"But don't worry. I asked my mom to email me about it. That way your dad doesn't have to worry about it when he's overwriting my memory."

"Hmm." Definitely falling asleep.

"Hey, Lucky. You can't fall asleep draped across me like a blanket. I'm going to need to pee soon." I shook her lightly.

She let out a disgruntled sound then released me. "But you're so cozy."

I kissed her forehead. "So you said."

The sleepy redhead gave me a sweet smile. "I think you're nifty."

"Nifty, huh? Is that something you look for in potential dates?"

"Maybe?" Her eyes drifted shut again.

I watched her like that for a long moment. "Hey, why don't you go lie down in the bed for a while? I'll wake you up. I promise."

"Nap with me?" Her voice was raspy and small, like a little kid who just woke up.

I laughed softly. "You and me in a bed together isn't conducive to sleep. That's why you're so tired."

"Worth it," she mumbled before letting go of me and settling on the other end of the couch. "I'll nap here."

"How long do you want me to let you sleep, woman?" I rubbed her feet. She really was sweet, too, on top of all her other amazing qualities.

"Half hour?" The words were muffled by the pillow she was hugging the same way she'd hugged me.

Chapter Eleven

When I got back from the bathroom, Lucky was snoring softly. I studied her sleeping form and marveled once again that this beautiful creature not only let me touch her, but begged me to. Instead of picking the book back up, I sat in her ratty old recliner and watched her. I remembered my responsibility as Lucky's alarm clock, set a reminder on my phone, then settled back into the comfort of this chair that smelled vaguely of my lover.

I had to figure out a way to keep her in my life. I wasn't in love with her, though the sex hangover hormones flooding my system were trying to tell me otherwise. I'd known her for less than a week, so love wasn't possible. Not yet. But there was the promise of something there between us, a possibility that it could grow into love, and I wanted to see where it could go.

My mind drifted to what could be. Other than the sex, there'd be companionship. Laughter and good food and someone who'd genuinely listen to me. I was lonely, had been for a while, but that wasn't new. I'd been lonely off and on—mostly on—since my divorce. For a while before it, too, if I were honest. I'd filled the space with work, but out of necessity. Working three part-time jobs didn't leave a lot of time for relationships. Lucky had come into my life at the perfect time, if only we hadn't had the bad luck or misjudgment or whatever that had led to her revealed truth.

A sigh I couldn't hold in escaped as I realized I'd probably end up with Sam now. A nice guy who my friends introduced me to wouldn't be the end of the world, but the spark I had with Lucky was so much better.

If only I'd stuck to my guns and left when I'd planned to that first night. She would have asked me for my phone number and I could be feeling the giddy euphoria of the beginning of something new instead of the gathering gloom of the ending of something lovely. If only we could start over, knowing what we knew. I sat up straight. That was an idea.

My phone buzzed, telling me it was time to wake Lucky from her nap, so I moved from the recliner to crouch next to Lucky. "Hey, sweet stuff. Time to wake up."

Her face was pressed into the back of the couch, and when I rubbed her back, she turned to face me, stretching. Her cheek had picked up the texture of the throw pillow. I traced my finger over the wrinkles.

"Hey," she said in her sleepy, hoarse voice. Lucky rubbed her cheek against my hand, like a cat. My heart gave an extra-strength thud.

"What if we start over after your father rewrites my memories? I could tell you about where I go in a typical week and you could find me. I was instantly attracted to you when we first met. You caught me staring, remember? I bet you could seduce me again."

Lucky went from half asleep to fully awake in the literal blink of an eye.

"Yes, we should do that. You want to do that?"

"Obviously. Why would I have suggested it if I didn't want to figure out a way to keep you in my life?" I grinned at her.

Suddenly, I was on my back on the floor. Lucky had tackled me and was kissing me breathless.

Eventually, she let up and grinned at me.

"Does this mean you've forgiven me?"

"There's nothing to forgive. You made an understandable mistake, and really, it was my fault, too. I could have left when I originally planned to. Or after you fucked me halfway to oblivion. I fell asleep in your arms just as much as you fell asleep holding me." I reached up to push the hair out of her face.

"There really is something here, isn't there?" Her tone was hopeful.

I nodded.

Lucky pressed her cheek to mine before getting up and pulling me off the floor. "Besides, it's not like we don't have people in common. I could ask Kim to introduce me to his cute colleague."

"Or Pat," I added. "Padraig knows the whole situation. He's the one who assured me that you did actually like me. That gave me the confidence to try something."

"Yeah?" Lucky gave me one of her infectious smiles. What could I do other than grin back?

My beautiful lover pulled me again, but this time it was over to the couch. She pushed me to sit, planted herself next to me, and then snuggled into my side. "If I'm going to have to wait a while to touch you again, I want to get as much of you as I can between now and when my dad comes back."

"Makes sense." I put my arm around her shoulders.

"Now, tell me, do you do your grocery shopping on any kind of schedule? Because I could flirt with you over whatever frozen abomination you're buying."

"What?" I leaned back to look at her and found her smirking.

"I may have looked in your fridge and freezer to see what kind of food you liked. I didn't pick baked ziti out of the air. Saw you have lots of frozen lasagna in your freezer." Lucky tilted her head as if waiting for me to challenge her.

Instead, I kissed her. A quick peck to tell her that I didn't care that she'd snooped.

"I usually go to the Wegmans in Pittsford on Sunday mornings. Or Sunday afternoons if the Bills are playing." She looked a little disheartened. I realized it was a big grocery store and it would be hard to engineer a seeming accidental encounter. But then I saved her. "I spend a lot of time at that coffee place just off campus in between semesters, Pittsford Roasters? They make great breakfast burritos, so I usually show up there shortly after they open and stay for a few hours. I like the ambient noise and can get a lot of work done."

"Oh, that cute one with the fireplace?"

I nodded, and she smiled.

"I've been there before. Plenty. Bear and Pat's place is just up the road."

"And since I have to finish prepping for a class I'm teaching starting the week after next, I'll be there every morning next week."

Her grin broadened. "I'll try to take seducing you seriously this time."

"Good," I whispered to her before closing the distance and kissing her softly but with obvious intent. "Now how about you take me seriously to bed? It's been, what, at least fourteen hours since my last orgasm?"

"Mmm." She licked at my lips. "You make a good point, my lady. But why waste time moving to the bedroom?"

Lucky disentangled herself from my embrace and pulled her shirt off. She had neglected to put a bra on this morning. I sucked in a breath.

"Two can play at that game," I told her. I had put on a bra—my back tended to hurt if I didn't wear a bra on a regular basis—but I'd put on one that was black lace. Revealing it had the desired effect. Lucky straddled my lap and kissed me fiercely.

I moved a hand between us so I could play with her oh-so-sensitive nipples and had just started towards that goal when there was a knock at Lucky's door.

"Are you expecting someone?" I whispered quietly, intent on not being heard.

"No. Sometimes people will come around back and knock on my door when they don't get an answer at the big house." She kissed me, softly. "Let's just be quiet until they go away."

I tried to listen for receding footsteps or some other sign that the person on the other side of the door had left, but Lucky distracted me by pulling down one of one of my bra straps and licking delicately along the mark it left on my shoulder.

"How can I stay quiet with you doing that?" I spoke the words directly into her ear and then nipped at her lobe.

The knocking came again, this time followed by a man's voice I didn't recognize. "Lucille Orla O'Quinn, are you alive? Or did that human harm you?"

Lucky sat back and looked at me, eyes wide. "That's my father."

"But he's not supposed to be back for another day!" I reached for my shirt as Lucky jumped off my lap and reached for hers.

"Two days," Lucky corrected me. She sounded like she was going to cry. "We were supposed to have more time!"

"I have a key and I'm going to let myself in, human, so you better not have hurt my girl," the man outside called, and the doorknob started to turn.

"Da, I'm fine," Lucky yelled as she rushed to the door. I had just gotten my shirt on when the door burst open, revealing a tall, dark-haired man who looked so much like Lucky that there was no mistaking him for anyone other than her father.

"What are you doing home early?" my lover asked nervously, looking between her father, me, and the audience we had—Shannon and Bear.

"What do you mean, 'What am I doing home early'? Your aunt sent me a missive and it found me right where I'd told her I'd be. My girl needed me. Of course I came home early." He stepped into the room and shot me a vicious glare.

Someone had missed a trick with naming. Here was a bear if ever I saw one. He towered over everyone in the room, and with his dark hair and thick beard, he was as intimidating as a Kodiak.

I noticed Shannon was smirking at me.

"Good afternoon, Mrs. Murphy." I pushed myself up from the couch and stood beside Lucky.

"And to you, Professor Rose." She ran her hand along her neck and then pointed to me. "You seem to have left your hair inside your shirt."

"Almost as if you put it on quickly because someone was about to barge in," Bear added with his own smirk. "Pat says hello. Said he had a lovely time with you and that he'll keep his promise to find you on the other side of this."

I fixed my hair and gave Bear a grateful nod.

Lucky took a half step back so we stood together and took my hand in hers. She squeezed it lightly and then lifted our joined hands to her lips for a soft kiss.

"Da, you didn't have to rush. You could get settled in the house first if you want. I know how grumpy you are when you first come back to the human realm." Lucky stood tall and didn't flinch away from the man.

Brian pulled his eyes away from our joined hands and looked me up and down. "Professor?"

"Yeah, she teaches..." Bear started.

"Did I ask you, Bearach?" Brian cut in.

"No, sir," Bear answered, but I could tell he was anything but contrite. His smirk turned into a full grin as I watched.

"I teach at Pittsford College. In the English department." This was the oddest 'meet the parent' moment I'd ever had, and I'd once dated first a brother and then a sister from the same family back when I was in undergrad.

"Bearach, doesn't your man work there, too? Shan, I thought you told me they met at The Warren?" Brian folded his arms over his impressively wide chest. Whoever first wrote all leprechauns were diminutive had no idea how wrong they were.

"We did meet there, sir." I answered him since he hadn't looked away from me yet.

One of his eyebrows quirked at my calling him 'sir.'

"Da, please can I have a little more time with her before you rewrite her memories?" Lucky had started bouncing on her feet and squirming. I hoped, silently, that she didn't ever try to play poker. She was so easy to read.

"I love you, my girl, but I'm not talking to you either." He let out a humph and then continued. "She's just your type, though, isn't she, Luck? Looks a bit like that doctor you dated before Billy died. Only the professor is prettier."

"Thank you?" I said after he stared at me for a long, long moment.

He moved to sit in a big, wingback chair next to the television. Brian O'Quinn looked like a king on his throne, and I felt even more intimidated.

"Sit." He gestured to the couch.

Lucky and I moved as one towards the couch, and her father sighed. "Just the professor. You can stay and listen, but I am not of a mood for your interfering. And don't you give me that look either, Shan."

Bear snickered from behind me. "Niss, I just noticed your shirt's on backwards."

I shot him a quick look and saw he was grinning at me unrepentantly.

"So," Lucky's father started as soon as I sat, "I assume you're the reason it smells like sex in here."

My cheeks went hot as I looked at the man.

"Da, can you please not embarrass me right now?" Lucky whined, then turned to me. "I'm sorry for..."

"Hush, Lucky."

"I..." I finally managed to push out a word, but he raised a hand to wave me off.

"My daughter is in her late forties. Her sex life or lack thereof is her business. I'm not going to burn you at the stake for taking her virtue or something equally vile and misogynistic." He leaned back in the chair.

"Yes, sir. I am sleeping with your daughter."

"Present tense," he commented.

His eyes moved off to my right. "When did you get a new phone, Lucky?"

"Oh!" was all she said.

I turned to see what he was looking at and saw my phone was still on the coffee table. "That's my phone, sir."

"Bearach, I thought you hid that." Shannon finally spoke again.

"I let her have it back," Lucky admitted.

The big man unleashed an angry string of Gaelic vulgarities while looking at his daughter.

"Da, you know I just started learning Irish Gaelic. Slow down if you want me to understand."

"He called you—" I stopped and sighed. "Well, it boils down to him questioning both the circumstances of your birth and the contents of your head."

Brian O'Quinn turned his attention back to me. In Gaelic, he asked, "You speak the tongue?"

"A bit," I said back in Gaelic before finishing in English. "I can read it fluently and mostly understand it when it's spoken, but I learned it for research reasons, so my pronunciation is awful and my American accent is obvious."

A small smile flitted across the big man's face, and he nodded before his attention went back to Lucky.

Brian's eyebrow quirked up. He started again, but calmly and in English this time. "Luck, my girl, you know the rules. Forgetting your spells because of a pretty girl, I understand. We went through this when you were a teen. Letting the human have access to the outside world is forbidden for a reason."

"Sir, I didn't tell anyone anything."

His dark brown eyes turned on me. "This time I wasn't talking to you."

"I trust her," Lucky answered immediately.

"Hmm," was Brian's only comment before he turned back to me. "I was under the impression that you wanted to get away from her as quickly as possible."

"That's how I felt at the beginning of all this. That's not how I feel now."

"And how do you feel now? Are you about to tell me you're in love with my Lucky? After only five days?"

I looked over at the woman in question then back at her father. "No, sir, I'm not. But I do like her a whole lot. She's funny and kind and smart. Before you showed up..."

"I know what you were doing before I showed up, professor."

I felt my cheeks heat again, but I smiled at the man. "Before that." I took a breath to calm myself. "Before that we were making plans for how we could meet again after you've done your magic on my memory."

"And what have you planned so you can make lightning strike twice?"

"With respect, that's between me and Lucky. You said it yourself: Her sex life or lack thereof is none of your business."

The three other people in the room collectively gasped, but Brian held my gaze steadily. "You want to date my daughter."

"Very much. And if we make it a year or two, you can put me through whatever ceremony and test me however you want."

Brian looked confused. "Ceremony?"

I looked to Lucky, who also looked confused. "Lucky said that when you and her mother were dating, there was a ceremony and a length of time and a few other requirements."

"Ah, no. The clan advises and the clan leader, meaning me at the moment, decides. My clan put Ginny—" He paused and looked to me. "That was Lucky's mother. My clan put her through all that because they were testing Ginny and my love for her. I swore then that if I became leader, I'd stop that nonsense."

"Oh." Lucky met my eyes, and I felt exactly as excited as she seemed.

"You're not a Catholic, are you?" Brian sounded like he was growling, making me think about bears again. "Not that I like Protestants much more. Catholics ruined Ireland in my opinion, and I never saw anyone more anxious to steal a 'chaun's gold."

I pulled my necklace out from my shirt and showed him the silver and turquoise hamsa I always wore. "No, sir. I was raised Jewish, though I'm really more agnostic than anything else."

"Oh, well," Brian said, leaning back in his chair, "that's good."

He looked around the room and let out an enormous sigh.

"What are your thoughts, sister?"

Shannon shrugged. "I like her. Besides, when was the last time you saw your daughter smiling like that?"

I looked and saw she wasn't wrong. Lucky was grinning, and it was beautiful. I held out my hand, and she grasped it in hers then came to sit next to me. "I like her, Da."

"And you, boy? Also, what's your husband think?"

"Same as my mam. Both of us." Bear winked at me.

"Well, that's a mark met." Brian slapped both hands down on his thighs and then stood. "Here's what I have to say about all this: I'm inclined to give you until when I was supposed to be back at the very least."

Lucky and I looked at each other, both grinning like fools.

"We'll have lunch together tomorrow. Lucky, Niss, and me. I want to get to know you a bit better before I make any kind of decision about what to do next. And if I like what I learn, we'll have more family over to see what the clan thinks."

"Da? What does it matter what the clan thinks?" Lucky voiced my question perfectly.

"Can't really know if she's trustworthy from you, now, can I? I'm trying really hard not to think about how much sex you must have had to make it stink like this in here. I know I get extra sensitive to everything human while I'm in Ayrie, but really. Anyway, you're not to be trusted, Luck. Or, you are, but I need more than your word." He crossed the room and shooed Shannon and Bear out of the way so he could open the door. "She can keep her memories—and her phone—for now. I want others to meet her before I make a decision about letting her keep them for good."

Brian pulled the door open and left before anything else could be said, and Shannon followed him. Bear hung back, grinning. "I'll cross my fingers for you and start working on the cousins. So happy for you, regardless."

When we were alone again, Lucky looked entirely flabbergasted.

"I guess your dad likes me?"

"I guess so." She grinned and then threw herself at me. "I like you, too, you know."

I laughed and folded my arms around her. "Good thing it runs in the family, huh?"

Epilogue

THREE MONTHS LATER

Standing in the exact spot where I'd been the first time I laid eyes on my girlfriend, watching her again, I couldn't help smiling. Keeping my memories 'for now' had been Brian's opinion for a while. At first, 'for now' was until I could meet the rest of the family. Then 'for now' was expanded and I was allowed to leave Lucky's home but I had to check in with Lucky—preferably in person—at least once a day. After he'd been home for a week, Lucky reminded him that if he was going to rewrite my memories, he had to do it now or not at all. Then Brian, bless him, said, "Fine. Not at all."

Lucky hadn't noticed me yet, so I took the opportunity to watch her move around behind the bar. I still couldn't believe that *she* wanted *me*.

"Have you told her yet?"

Shannon startled me out of my reverie. I turned to look at the woman, searching her face. She wasn't so intimidating now that I knew her better.

"Told her what?"

"That you're in love with her. Obviously." The older woman grinned up at me. That was another thing I hadn't noticed back when we first met: I was a lot taller than Shannon.

"Hhhhow?" I stared at her, flabbergasted. I'd only just realized that the affection and like I felt for Lucky had grown. Just that morning, as I watched her sleeping in my bed, after I got up to go teach. The morning sun splashing across her back and on her sleep-rumpled face made it feel like my heart was too big for my chest. I'd woken her up to tell her and ended up being late because she pulled me back into bed.

"Your pupils might as well be heart shaped, like in a cartoon, the way you were just looking at her." Shannon bumped me with her shoulder. "Always did like you. Ever since you stood up to me about her ridiculous nickname. Have you introduced her to your parents yet?"

"Yes, and they like her. They don't like that she's not Jewish, but they like her."

I turned to look over at Lucky, who had finally noticed me. She raised a hand in greeting and gave me one of her heart-stopping smiles.

"That's what you look like. Exact same expression." Shannon whispered before pushing me towards the bar.

"Hello, muh khree," Lucky said when I got to the bar.

"More Irish Gaelic, huh? Your accent is so much better than mine."

She grinned and poured me a glass of wine without my having to ask.

"You know what it means, right?" I asked her. I knew that sometimes Bear or Shannon would feed Lucky phrases without explaining them, just to see if I would catch on.

There was a stutter in her movements as she pushed the glass towards me. A faint blush took over her cheeks. "Um, well…" She looked down then up again and met my eyes. "It means 'my heart'."

I reached over the bar and put my hand atop hers where it rested. "You know my accent is rubbish, and I don't know how to say anything like that in Hebrew or Yiddish, so how about I just call you 'my love'?"

Lucky lifted my hand and kissed the back of it. "That works for me."

"Guess you're not as unlucky in love as you thought you were. Or maybe you were saving it up for me." I pulled the main reason I was here tonight out of my pocket and held it out to her.

It wasn't a surprise—we'd discussed it a couple of days earlier—but she still beamed at me.

She took out her overloaded keychain and immediately added the key to my apartment. Lucky rubbed her finger over the key before coming around the bar. She turned my stool around so she could stand between my legs. Lucky cupped my cheeks and kissed me gently.

"I'll have a copy of mine made for you in the morning."

"You sure Brian will be okay with that?" I looped my arms around her and pulled Lucky closer.

"He suggested it a couple of weeks ago, but I didn't want to be pushy."

I rested my forehead against hers. "I love you," I whispered.

"I love you, too," she responded.

I kissed her again, but we got interrupted by a wolf whistle.

We pulled apart and I grinned over at Padraig, who was the other reason I was there. We were having dinner together since both Bear and Lucky were working.

"Get a room, you two!" He started to move towards a table, then turned back to us. "By the way, Angela is running late, but she'll be here."

Lucky flipped Pat the bird and gave me another quick kiss. "Definitely saved all my luck up for you."

THE END

Afterword

If you love Niss and Lucky (and Shannon and Bear) as much as I do, please consider reviewing *Getting Lucky* on Amazon, Goodreads, LibraryThing, or social media, or even just tell a friend you think will appreciate steamy sex between a lonely literature professor and an even lonelier bartender.

Make sure to head to my website, jessicaolin.com, to see what else I'm working on and to sign up for my newsletter. Subscribers get previews of future works, extended snippets of works in progress, and—most importantly—exclusive pictures of my own feline overlords.

Connect with me on social media:

- Bluesky: @olinj
- Tumblr: library-graffiti

Thanks for reading!

Acknowledgements

Supriya, Susanah, and Liz, for beta reading early versions. And to Liz again, for basically daring me to write this when I complained about another leprechaun romance.

About the Author

Jessica Olin grew up either thirty minutes or two hours north of Boston, depending on traffic. They spent a lot of their childhood dreaming up love stories both for themselves and others—including Real Person Fiction about their junior high celebrity crush,Simon Le Bon! They read their first romance novel as a teenager and immediately decided that they wanted to be a romance novelist when they grew up. Life and a strong drive to be practical took them away from that dream, through three different college degrees, four major career changes, and eight different states, until they realized they had the right idea at thirteen and started writing romance again. They currently live in a house that is constantly in need of repair with a criminal mastermind cat and a cat who has no thoughts in his head, only purrs. Jessica also has a grab-bag of identities—Jewish, queer, fat, and neuro-atypical—that are sorely underrepresented in romance, and they are determined to change that.

Also By

Getting My Goat

Getting your goat can sometimes lead to love.

Maya Applebaum is doing okay. Now. She got laid off from her job teaching software design at a community college, but she managed to find a role designing educational games at a company where she gets to work from home. She's living like a nun—kind of funny, since she's Jewish—but she has her job and her friends and Nimoy, her former alley-cat-turned-cosseted-house-pet. Everything is okay.

Okay, that is, until she lands in bed with her neighbor and landlord, Leander Costas, who turns out to be not so human after all. Leander also turns out to be the most amazing cook, friend, and lover Maya's ever known. When Maya is put in danger because of someone from his past, Leander faces down the threats to her life. But only she can face down the threat of a broken heart.

Read the first chapter Tumblr.

Buy the book on Amazon.

Coming Soon

Book 3 in the

"Monstrous Rochester" series

Howl Stand By You

Fiona Morrison lives a simple life. They go to work, hang out with a few friends, spend time with a few relatives. The best part of their week is their Saturday visits to the farmers market. Sure, they're there to pick up groceries, but they're also there to ogle one of the vendors: Malachi "Kai" Hunter. Kai is the owner of Hunter's Glen, a farm that produces the best goat cheese Fiona's ever eaten. He's also soft spoken and kind and he's got the prettiest light brown eyes. Fiona's got it bad for the handsome farmer but is content to leave things as they are. Content, that is, until Kai is forced to reveal that he's a werewolf because he needs Fiona's help. Their mutual attraction quickly brings them together in a passionate affair, but circumstances are conspiring to keep them apart.